HIS FOREVER FAMILY

SARAH M. ANDERSON

ISBN-13: 978-0-373-73438-2

His Forever Family

Copyright © 2016 by Sarah M. Anderson

Never Too Late
Copyright © 2006 by Harlequin Books S.A.
Brenda Jackson is acknowledged as the author of this work.

Recycling programs for this product may not exist in your area.

Printed in U.S.A.

www.Harlequin.com

She was doing this, she really was.

She was crossing that little line and getting into an elevator with Marcus.

"Okay?" he asked as the doors slid shut, blocking them off from the bright lobby. He slid his arm around her waist and pulled her in close. "Still okay?"

In her dreams, Marcus swept into the office and kissed her and told her how much he needed her and yes, they wound up in bed.

But in those dreams, Marcus was the one doing all the sweeping. She didn't do anything but let herself get carried away in the over-the-top romance of the whole situation.

This was stupid. This wasn't just a risk—this was practically career suicide. Yes, she wanted Marcus and yes, he wanted her, and thank God they were both unattached, consenting adults.

It didn't change the fact that she was initiating a physical relationship with her boss. It didn't change the fact that she'd kissed him back.

But there was no going back to the way things were.

"Better than okay," she said, pulling him down for a kiss.

Marcus's lips moved over hers as he spun and backed her against the wall of the elevator.

* * *

His Forever Family
is part of Harlequin Desire's #1 bestselling series
Billionaires and Babies:
Powerful men...wrapped around
their babies' little fingers

Dear Reader,

Welcome to Chicago—a big city with big dreams and big money. Marcus Warren has it all—he's the heir to the Warren fortune and he's made his own several times over. But appearances can be deceiving—Marcus struggles to feel as if he's in control of his own life. His parents put an incredible amount of pressure on him to protect the Warren family name.

His favorite part of the day is when he runs with his assistant, Liberty Reese. She's something rare in his world—honest and loyal. Her faith in him is the one thing Marcus's billions can't buy.

Liberty, however, has secrets of her own. She's hidden her poverty-stricken childhood—and her criminal mother—for years in order to survive, and that's exactly what she's done. She's got a good job, a good boss and she's not living on the ragged edge anymore.

Until the morning she and Marcus find an abandoned baby boy on their morning run. As they bond with the baby, everything between them changes. Marcus is finally ready to fight for someone he wants. But when he finds out Liberty's been lying to him the entire time, will he turn his back on his forever family?

His Forever Family is a sensual story about accepting your past and choosing your future. I hope you enjoy reading this book as much as I enjoyed writing it! Be sure to stop by sarahmanderson.com and sign up for my newsletter at eepurl.com/nv39b for all the latest on my new releases!

Sarah

CONTENTS

Award-winning author **Sarah M. Anderson** may live east of the Mississippi River, but her heart lies out west on the Great Plains. With a lifelong love of horses and two history teachers for parents, it wasn't long before her characters found themselves out in South Dakota among the Lakota Sioux.

Sarah's book *A Man of Privilege* won the *RT Book Reviews* 2012 Reviewers' Choice Best Book Awards Series: Desire. Her book *Straddling the Line* was named Best Desire of 2013 by *CataRomance*, and *Mystic Cowboy* was a 2014 BBA Finalist in the Single Title category as well as a finalist for the Gayle Wilson Award of Excellence.

When not helping out at her son's school or walking her rescue dogs, Sarah spends her days having conversations with imaginary cowboys and American Indians, all of which is surprisingly well-tolerated by her wonderful husband. Readers can find out more about Sarah's love of cowboys and Indians at sarahmanderson.com.

Books by Sarah M. Anderson

Harlequin Desire

The Nanny Plan
His Forever Family

The Bolton Brothers

Straddling the Line
Bringing Home the Bachelor
Expecting a Bolton Baby

The Beaumont Heirs

Not the Boss's Baby
Tempted by a Cowboy
A Beaumont Christmas
His Son, Her Secret
Falling for his Fake Fiancé

Visit the Author Profile page
at Harlequin.com for more titles.

HIS FOREVER
FAMILY

Sarah M. Anderson

To Sasha Devlin, my Spring Fling buddy.
We'll always have Chicago!
And when we don't,
we'll always have Twitter!

One

"Come on, Ms. Reese," Marcus Warren called over his shoulder. "It's not that hot."

He paused in the middle of the jogging path to wait for his executive assistant, Liberty Reese, to catch up with him. He looked around, checking for any vans with dark windows that didn't belong. It was an old habit, keeping an eye out for danger. But as usual, aside from some other runners, he and Ms. Reese had the shoreline to themselves. Thank God. The past was in the past, he repeated to himself until his anxiety faded.

Man, he loved Lake Michigan. The early-morning light made the rippling water a deep blue. The sky was clear and warmed by the sun, which seemed to hover just about a foot over the surface of the water. Later today, the heat would be oppressive, but right now, running along the lakefront with a cool breeze blowing in from the water?

This was as close to free as Marcus got to feel.

He checked his Fitbit. His heart rate was falling. "You're not going to let the heat beat you, are you, Ms. Reese?" he teased, stretching out his quads.

Ms. Reese puffed up next to him. "May I take a moment to point out—again—that you're not taking notes while you run?" she said, glaring at him.

But he wasn't fooled. He saw the way the corner of her lips curved up as she said it. She was trying not to smile.

He kept stretching so she could catch her breath. "But I'm talking. That counts for something, right?"

She rolled her eyes and finished off the water. That made him grin. He was Marcus Warren, heir to his father's Warren Investments financial empire *and* his mother's Marquis Hotel empire. He was the sole owner of Warren Capital, a venture capital firm he'd started with his trust-fund money. He owned half of the Chicago Blackhawks and a quarter of the Chicago Bulls, in addition to 75 percent of the pro soccer team, the Chicago Fire. He was one of the richest bachelors in the country and possibly the richest one in Chicago.

People simply did not roll their eyes at him.

Except for Ms. Reese.

She tucked the bottle back into her belt. Then, her fingers hovering over the Bluetooth earpiece she wore at all times, she asked, "So how do you want to proceed with the watchmakers?"

Rock City Watches was a boutique firm that had set up shop in downtown Detroit and wanted a fresh round of investing to expand its operations. Marcus looked at his watch, made just for him. The 24-karat gold casing was warm against his skin. "What do you think?"

Ms. Reese sighed heavily and began to plod up the jogging path again. She was not a particularly graceful runner—*plodding* was the only word for it—but she kept up with him and took notes while they ran. It was the most productive time of day. He did his best thinking while they ran.

Which was why they ran every single day, in rain or heat. Ice was about the only thing that kept them indoors, but he had a treadmill in a room off his office. Ms. Reese could sit at a small desk and record everything and provide her opinion.

He let her get a few feet ahead of him. No, she was not terribly graceful. But that didn't stop him from admiring the view. Ms. Reese had curves—more than enough curves to give a man pause.

He shook his head, pushing all thoughts of her backside from his mind. He was not the kind of billionaire who slept with his secretary. His father had done that enough for both of them. Marcus's relationship with Ms. Reese was strictly business. Well, business and running.

He caught up to her easily. "Well?"

"No one wears watches anymore," she panted. "Unless it's a smart watch."

"Excellent point. I'll invest twenty-five million in Rock City Watches."

Ms. Reese stumbled a bit in surprise. Marcus reached out and steadied her. He didn't allow his hand to linger on her warm skin. "You okay? We're almost to the fountain." Buckingham Fountain was the point where they turned around and headed back.

She gave him a hell of a side eye. "I'm fine. How did you get from *timepieces are a dead market* to *let's invest another twenty-five million*?"

"If no one wears watches anymore, then they become what they once were—a status symbol," he explained. "Only the wealthiest consumers can afford a watch that costs several grand. The timepiece market isn't dead, Ms. Reese. The mass-market timepiece market is. But the luxury timepiece market?" He held out his wrist. "It's a hell of a nice watch, don't you think?" This particular watch went for $4,500.

She nodded. "It'll be great PR, as well. Made in America and all that."

"But they need to accept the realities of the market."

She nodded. "Such as?"

"Marketing and wearables. Let's get back to the Rock City Watch people with requests to see their marketing mock-ups. I also want to set up a meeting to discuss a hybrid device—a luxury watch that can slot wearable tech into the band."

They reached the fountain and she stopped, her head down and her hands on her knees as she took in great gulps of air.

"What else?" he asked.

"You have to make a decision about attending the Hanson wedding," she said in between gasps.

Marcus groaned. "Do I have to?"

"You're the one who decided you should go to this wedding," she told him flatly. "You're the one who decided you should take a date. And you're the one who decided to kill two birds with one stone by scheduling the meeting with the producers of *Feeding Frenzy* the day after the wedding."

Marcus allowed himself to scowl at his assistant. Her lack of sympathy was not comforting. Attending the Hanson-Spears wedding in Los Angeles had not, in fact, been his idea. Who the hell wanted to watch his former fiancée get married to the man she'd cheated on him with? Not him.

But his mother had decreed that Marcus would attend the wedding with a date and put on a happy face so they could "put this unfortunate event behind them." Of course, if his mother had had her way, Marcus would have married Lillibeth Hanson anyway because what was a little affair in the grand scheme of things? Lillibeth came from old money. Marcus came from old money and made new money. Together, his parents had reasoned, they could apparently rule the world.

Marcus didn't see the point. He'd refused to reconcile with Lillibeth and he'd thought his parents had accepted that decision. But then the wedding invitation came.

And the hell of it was, his parents were not entirely wrong about the effects the scandal had had on Marcus's business. To some, his inability to see the truth about Lillibeth until it was too late might also indicate an inability to make good investment choices. So his parents had strongly suggested he attend the wedding to show that everyone was on good terms. And they *strongly* suggested he take a date because it would be an admission of defeat to show up at your ex's wedding alone.

All Marcus had to do was pick a woman.

He looked at Liberty. "What are my options, again?"

"Rosetta Naylor."

Marcus cringed at the celebutante's name. "Too shallow."

"Katerine Nabakov."

"Too Russian Mafia."

Liberty sighed heavily. "Emma Green?"

Marcus scowled harder. He had actually gone out with Emma several times. "Really?"

"She's a known quantity," Liberty explained. "No surprises."

"Wrong. People would think that us dating again is a sure sign of wedding bells." Specifically, his parents.

Marcus had done many things to keep the peace with his mother and father. Hell, he'd come damn close to getting married to Lillibeth Hanson, all because they thought that was best.

He wasn't going to risk that kind of trap again.

"The options are limited and time is running short, Mr. Warren," Liberty said in exasperation. She jammed her hands on her hips. "The wedding is in two weeks. If you insist on attending with a date, you need to actually ask someone to go with you."

"Fine. I'll just take you."

The effect of this statement was immediate. Liberty's eyes went wide and her mouth dropped open and, in a fraction of a second, her gaze dropped over his body. Something that looked a hell of a lot like *want* flashed over her face.

What? Did she actually *want* him?

Then it was gone. She straightened up and did her best to look imperial. "Mr. Warren, be serious."

"I am serious. I trust you." He took a step toward her. "Sometimes I think…you're the only person who's honest with me. You wouldn't try to sell all the details of a date to the gossip rags." Which had been a huge part of the scandal with Lillibeth. She had capitalized on her affair, painting Marcus as a lousy boyfriend both in and out of the bedroom.

Liberty bit at her lower lip. "Honestly? I don't think you should go at all. Why would you give her the chance to hurt you again?" Her voice had dropped and she didn't sound imperial at all. Instead, she sounded…as if she wanted to protect him.

It was a fair question. He didn't want to go. He didn't want to give Lillibeth the chance to cut him down again. But he'd promised his parents that he'd put a good face on it and make sure the Warren name still meant power and money.

"And for the record," she went on, "I think doing that *Feeding Frenzy* reality show is also a bad idea. The whole problem with Lillibeth was that your private life suddenly became public fodder. Going on television to bid on investment ideas? You're just inviting people to further make a commodity out of you."

"It's supposed to be a good way to build my brand."

Liberty rolled her eyes again, as if that was the stupidest thing she'd ever heard. "Seriously? You've built a successful venture capital firm without being a celebrity. You have plenty of people dying to pitch to you. Heck, I'm surprised we haven't been accosted by a 'jogger' lying in wait to pitch you his million-dollar idea yet."

He tensed at the idea of being accosted by anyone. But no—no suspicious vehicles with armed men were around. The past was in the past.

"But you know what?" Liberty took a step toward him, jabbing at him with her index finger. She could be a formidable woman in her own right. "You do this reality show, that's exactly what's going to happen. You won't be able to run along the lake without plowing through idiots in running shoes who want a piece of your time and your fortune. Don't feed the machine, Marcus. Don't do what 'they' think you should do. For the love of God, do what *you* want."

Marcus. Had she ever called him by his first name before? He didn't think so. The way her lips moved over his name—that was the sort of thing he'd remember. "Maybe I want to take you to the wedding."

It was hard to say if she blushed, as she was already red faced from the run and the heat. But something in her expression changed. "No," she said flatly. Before he could take the rejection personally, she added, "I—it—would be bad for you."

He could hear the pain in her voice. He took a step toward her and put a hand on her shoulder. She looked up, her eyes wide and—hopeful? His hand drifted from her shoulder to her cheek and damned if she didn't lean into his touch. "How could you be bad for me?"

The moment the words left his mouth, he realized he'd pushed this too far. Yes, Liberty Reese was an exceptional assistant and yes, she was beautiful—when she wasn't struggling through a summer run.

But what had started as an offhand comment about a date to a wedding now meant something else. Something more.

She shut down on him. She stepped out of his touch and turned to face the lake. "It's getting warmer," she said in a monotone voice. "We need to finish our run."

"Do you have any water left?"

She looked sheepish. "No."

He held out his hand. "Give me your bottle. There's a water fountain a couple hundred yards away. I'll fill it up."

She unhooked her bottle and handed it over. "Thanks," she said, sounding perfectly normal, as if he hadn't just asked her out and touched her face. As if she hadn't turned him down flat. Somehow, it made him admire her even more. "I'll wait here. Try not to get any brilliant ideas, okay?"

Marcus took off at top speed. He heard Liberty shout, "Show-off!"

He laughed.

The water in the drinking fountain was too warm. He let it run for a few seconds, hoping it'd cool off. As he waited, he looked around. There was a trash can only a few feet away, boxes and bags piled around it on the ground. Marcus scowled at the garbage. Why couldn't people take care of the park, dammit? The trash can was right there.

As he filled the water bottle and debated calling the mayor about the garbage pickup schedule, he heard a noise. It was a small noise, but it didn't belong. It wasn't a gull crying or a squirrel scampering—it was closer to a...a cat mewing?

Marcus looked around, trying to find the source of the noise. A shoe box on the ground next to the trash can moved.

Marcus's stomach fell in. Oh, no—who would throw a kitten away? He hurried over to the box and pulled the lid off and—

Sweet Jesus. Not a cat. Not a kitten.

A *baby*.

Two

Breathing hard, Liberty admired the view as Marcus sprinted away from her. When he reached the water fountain, she turned her attention back to the lake. It wouldn't do to be caught staring at her boss's ass. Even if it was a *fine* ass. And even if the owner had just made one of himself.

Instead, she took the time to appreciate the gift that was this morning. She hadn't set foot in a church in a good fifteen years. But every morning she stood here and looked out on Lake Michigan and gave thanks to God or the higher power or whoever the hell was listening.

She was alive. She was healthy. She had a good job that paid for food and a safe apartment. There was even some money left over for things like running shoes and haircuts.

"Liberty?" Marcus yelled from the water fountain. "Liberty!"

Even though Marcus couldn't see her, she glared at him. What the hell had gotten into him this morning? One of the

reasons she worked for him—aside from the insane salary
he paid her—was the fact that he treated her as an equal.
It was a bit of delusion on her part to pretend that she was
on par with the likes of Marcus Warren, but it was her delusion, dammit.

And that delusion worked only because it was just her
and Marcus on these runs, both in running clothes. The delusion didn't work when he was wearing a four-thousand-
dollar suit and she had on the finest suit she could find on
80 percent clearance at Macy's. And the delusion sure as
hell wouldn't work if she accompanied him to a three-day
destination wedding extravaganza that no doubt cost more
than she'd ever earn in her lifetime.

Someone would see through her facade. It'd get ugly, fast.

"Liberty!" He was even louder this time.

Was he not used to women saying no to him? Oh, whom
was she kidding? Women didn't say no to him. Why would
they? He was gorgeous, single, richer than sin and eminently
respectable. "What?"

"I need you!" he yelled over his shoulder. "Hurry!"

She realized he wasn't standing at the water fountain
anymore. He was on his knees by a trash can in the gravel
that surrounded the fountain. His shoulders were hunched
over and he looked as if—oh, God, he wasn't having a heart
attack, was he?

Liberty began to hurry. The three years of daily morning
runs with Marcus had given her enough stamina that she
broke into a flat-out run.

"Are you okay?" she demanded as she came up to him.
"Marcus—what's wrong?"

He looked up at her, his eyes wide with fear and one hand
over his mouth. Just then, something in front of him made
a pitiful little noise.

She looked down. What she saw didn't make sense at

first. There was a box and inside was something small and dark and moving.

"Baby?" Marcus said in a strangled voice.

"Baby!" Liberty cried with a start. She didn't know much about babies, but this child couldn't be more than a week old. The baby was wrapped in a filthy rag, and dark smudges that might have been dirt but were more the color of dried blood covered its dark skin. Wisps of black hair were plastered to its tiny little head. Liberty stared in total shock, trying to make sense of it: an African American newborn in a shoe box by the trash can.

"It was—the box—it was closed," Marcus began to babble. "And I heard a noise and—baby. Baby!"

The baby opened its little mouth and let out another cry, louder this time. The sound broke Liberty out of her shock. Jesus Christ, someone had tried to throw this baby away! In a box in this heat? "Move," she commanded and Marcus dutifully scooted out of her way.

Her hands shaking, Liberty lifted the baby out of the box. The rag fell away from the impossibly tiny body—no diaper. A boy, and he was caked in filth.

"Oh, my God," she whispered as the baby's back arched and it let out a squeal. His little body was like a furnace in her hands.

"What do we do?" Marcus asked. He was clearly panicking.

And Liberty couldn't blame him. "Water," she realized. "He's too hot."

Marcus held out her water bottle, the one he'd been filling. She grabbed the rag and said, "Soak that in the fountain," and took her bottle.

The baby squirmed mightily in her arms and she had this moment that was almost an out-of-body thing, where instead of looking down at a little baby boy she'd just plucked from a shoe box, she was looking down at William, the baby brother she'd never gotten the chance to see, much less hold. Was this what he'd been like, after their mother gave birth in prison and the baby was taken away to a foster home? Had William died like this?

No. This baby, whoever he was, was not going to die. Not if she had anything to do with it.

"This is disgusting," Marcus said, but she didn't pay any attention to him.

She folded herself into a cross-legged position on the gravel, ignoring the way the rocks dug into her skin. "It's okay," she soothed as she tried to dribble some water into the baby's mouth. "You're a good boy, aren't you? Oh, you're such a sweetheart." The baby turned his head from side to side and wailed piteously. Panic gripped her. What if he wasn't going to make it? What if she couldn't save him? "You're loved," she told him, tears coming to her eyes. "And you're so strong. You can do this, okay?"

"Here," Marcus said, thrusting the rag at her. Except it wasn't the rag—it was his shirt.

She looked up and found herself staring right at Marcus Warren's bare chest. In any other circumstances she would have taken her time admiring the view because *damn*. He was muscled and cut—but still lean. He had a true runner's body.

The baby whimpered. Right. She had much more important things to deal with than her boss suddenly half-naked. She held the baby away from her body. "Drape it over him."

Marcus did as he was told, laying the sopping-wet cloth over the baby's body. The sudden temperature change made the poor thing howl. "It's okay," she murmured to him, trying to get a little water into his mouth. "You'll feel better soon."

"Should I go for help? What should we do?"

Help. That would be a good thing. "My phone is in my pack," she said. He didn't run with his phone—that was her job. "Call 911." She was amazed at how calm she sounded, as if finding a baby on the verge of heatstroke in the trash was just another Tuesday in her life.

Marcus crouched behind her and dug through the fanny pack that held her water, keys and phone. "Got it." She told him her password without a second thought and he dialed. "We're at Buckingham Fountain and we found a baby in the trash," Marcus said way too loudly into the phone.

"Shh, shh," Liberty soothed as Marcus talked to the 911 dispatcher. "Here, let's try this." She dipped her finger into the water and held it against the baby's mouth. He sucked at it eagerly and made a little protest when she pulled her finger away to dip it into the water again.

He latched on to her finger a second time—which had the side benefit of cutting off the crying. Liberty took a deep breath and tried to think. There'd been a baby at her second foster home. How had the foster mother calmed that baby down?

Oh, yes. She remembered now. She began to rock back and forth, the gravel cutting into her legs. "That's a good boy," she said, her ears straining for the sounds of sirens. "You're loved. You can do it."

Agonizingly long minutes passed. She couldn't get the baby to take much more water, but he sucked on the tip of her finger fiercely. As she rocked and soothed him, his body relaxed and he curled up against her side. Liberty held him even tighter.

"Is he okay?" Marcus demanded.

She looked up at him, trying not to stare at his body. Never in the three years she'd worked for Marcus had she seen him even half this panicked. "I think he fell asleep. The poor thing. He can't be more than a few days old."

"How could anyone just leave him?" Now, that was more like the Marcus she knew—frustrated when the world did not conform to his standards.

"You'd be surprised," she mumbled, dropping her gaze back to the baby, who was still ferociously tugging on her finger in his sleep. Aside from being hot and filthy, he looked healthy. Of course, she'd never seen William before he died in foster care, so she didn't know what a drug-addicted newborn looked like. This child's head was round and his eyes were still swollen; she'd seen pictures of newborns who looked like him. She just couldn't tell.

"You're just about perfect, you know?" she told the infant. Then she said to Marcus, "Here, wet your shirt again. I think he's cooling down."

Marcus did as he was told. "You're doing an amazing job," he said as she wrapped the wet cloth around the baby's body. The baby started at the temperature change, but didn't let go of her finger. Marcus went on, "I didn't know you knew so much about babies," and she didn't miss the awe in his voice.

There's a lot you don't know about me. But she didn't say it because it'd been less than—what, twenty minutes? If that. It'd been less than twenty minutes since Marcus Warren had said he trusted her because she was the one person who was honest with him.

She wasn't—honest with him, that was. But that didn't mean she wanted to lie outright to him. She hated lying at all but she did what she had to do to survive.

So, instead, she said, "Must be the mothering instinct." What else could it be? Here was a baby who needed her in a truly primal way and Liberty had responded.

The baby sighed in what she hoped was contentment and she felt her heart clinch. "Such a good boy," she said, leaning down to kiss his little forehead.

Sirens came screaming toward them. Then the paramedics were upon them and everything happened *fast*. The baby was plucked from her arms and carried into the ambulance, where he wailed even louder. It tore her up to hear him cry like that.

At the same time, a police officer arrived and took statements from her and Marcus. Liberty found herself half listening to the questions as she stood at the back of the open ambulance while the medics dug out a pacifier and wrapped the baby in a clean blanket.

"Is he going to be okay?" she asked when one of the paramedics hopped out of the back and started to close the door.

"Hard to say," the man said.

"Where are you taking him?"

"Northwestern is closest."

Marcus broke off talking with the cop to say, "Take him to Children's." At some point, he'd put his shirt back on. It looked far worse for wear.

The paramedic shrugged and closed the doors, cutting Liberty off from the baby. The ambulance drove off—lights flashing but no sirens blaring.

The cop finished taking their statements. Liberty asked, "Will you be able to find the mother?"

Much like the paramedic, the cop shrugged. She supposed she shouldn't have been surprised. After all, she'd barely survived childhood because, aside from Grandma Devlin, people couldn't be bothered to check on little Liberty Reese. "It's a crime to abandon a baby," he said. "If the mother had left the baby at a police station, that's one thing. But…" He shrugged again. "Don't know if we'll find her, though. Usually babies are dumped close to where they're born, and someone in the neighborhood knows something. But the middle of the park?" He turned, as if the conversation was over.

"What'll happen to the baby?" Marcus asked, but Liberty could have told him.

If they couldn't find the mother or the father, the baby would go into the foster system. He'd be put up for adoption, eventually, but that might take a while until his case was closed. And by then, he might not be the tiny little baby he was right now. He might be bigger. And he was African American. That made it that much harder to get adopted.

She looked in the direction the ambulance had gone.

The cop gave Marcus a sad smile. "DCFS will take care of it," he said.

Liberty cringed. She did not have warm and fuzzy memories of the Department of Child and Family Services. All she had were grainy memories of frazzled caseworkers who couldn't be bothered. Grown-up Liberty knew that was because the caseworkers were overwhelmed by the sheer number of kids in the system. But little-kid Liberty only remembered trying to ask questions about why her mom or even Grandma Devlin wasn't going to come get her and being told, "Don't worry about it," as if that would make up for her mother's sudden disappearances.

What would happen to the baby? She looked at her arms, wondering at how empty they felt. "Marcus," she said in a hoarse voice as the cop climbed into his cruiser. "We can't lose that baby."

"What?" He stared at her in shock.

She grabbed on to his arm as if she was drowning and he was the only thing that could keep her afloat. "The baby. He'll get locked into the system and by the time the police close his case, it might be too late."

Marcus stared down at her as if she'd started spouting Latin. "Too…late? For what?"

Liberty's mouth opened and the words *I was a foster kid—trust me on this* almost rolled off her tongue. But at the last second, she snapped her mouth shut. She'd created this person Marcus saw, this Liberty Reese—a white college graduate, an excellent manager of time and money who always did her research and knew the answers. Liberty Reese was invaluable to Marcus because she had *made* herself valuable.

That woman had had nothing in common with Liberty Reese—the grubby daughter of an African American drug addict who'd sold herself on Death Corner in Cabrini-Green to afford more drugs, who'd done multiple stints in prison, who hadn't been able to get clean when her daughter was shipped back to foster care for the third time, who couldn't tell Liberty who her father was or even if he was white, who'd given birth to a baby boy addicted to heroin and crack and God only knew what else.

That's not who Liberty was anymore. She would never be that lost little girl ever again.

She looked back in the direction the ambulance had gone. That little baby—he was lost, too. Just as her brother had been in the few weeks he'd been alive. Completely alone in the world, with no one to fight for him.

Liberty would *not* allow that to happen. Not again.

She opened her mouth to tell Marcus something—she wasn't quite sure what, but something—except nothing came out. Her throat closed up and tears burned in her eyes.

Oh, God—was she about to start crying? No—*not* allowed. Liberty Reese did not cry. She was always in control. She never let her emotions get the better of her. Not anymore.

Marcus looked down at her, concern written large on his face. He stepped closer to her and cupped her chin. "Liberty…"

"Please," she managed to get out. "The baby, Marcus." But that was all she could say because then she really did begin to cry. She dropped her gaze and swallowed hard, trying to will the stupid tears back.

The next thing she knew, Marcus had wrapped his arms around her and pulled her into his chest. "It's okay," he murmured, his hand rubbing up and down her back. "The baby's going to be fine."

"You don't know that," she got out, trying to keep herself from sinking against his chest because Marcus Warren holding her? Comforting her?

The feeling, the smell of his body—awareness of Marcus as a man—blindsided her. Want, powerful and unexpected, mixed in with the panic over the baby and left her so confused that she couldn't pull away like she needed to and couldn't wrap her arms around him like she wanted to. She was rooted to the spot, wanting more and knowing she couldn't have it.

Marcus leaned back and tilted her head up so that she had no choice but to look him in the eyes. It wasn't fair, she thought dimly as she stared into the deep blue eyes that were almost exactly the same color as Lake Michigan on a clear day. Why couldn't he be a slimeball? Why did he have to be so damned perfect, hot and rich and now this—this *tenderness*? Why did he have to make her want him when she didn't deserve him?

He swiped his thumb over her cheek, brushing away a tear she hadn't been able to hold back. "It's important to you?" he asked, his voice deep. "The baby?"

"Yes," was all she could say, because what else was there? Marcus Warren was holding her in his arms and comforting her and looking at her as if he'd do anything to make her happy and dammit all if this wasn't one of her fantasies playing out in real life.

"Then I'll make it fine," he said. His thumb stroked over her cheek again and his other hand flattened out on her lower back. One corner of his mouth curved up into a smile that she knew well—the smile said that Marcus Warren was going to get exactly what he wanted.

And although she knew she shouldn't—couldn't—she leaned into his palm and let herself enjoy the sensation of Marcus touching her. "You will? Why would you do that for me?"

Something shifted in his eyes and his head dropped toward hers. He was going to kiss her, she realized. Her boss was going to kiss her and she was not only going to let him, she was going to kiss him back. Years of wanting and ignoring that want seemed to fall away.

But he didn't. Instead, he said, "Because you're important to me."

She forgot how to breathe. Heck, she might have forgotten her own name there for a second, because she was important to him. Not just a valuable employee. She, Liberty Reese, was important.

The alarm on her phone chimed, startling them out of whatever madness they'd been lost in. Marcus dropped his hand from her face and took a step away before he handed her phone to her. In all that had happened, she'd forgotten he had it.

It was eight forty-five? They'd started their morning run at seven. "You have a phone call with Dombrowski about that proposed bioenergy plant in fifteen minutes," she told him. Despite the heat that was building, she felt almost chilled without Marcus's arms around her.

Marcus laughed. "We're a little off schedule today. We haven't even showered."

Liberty froze as the image of the two of them in the shower together barged into her mind. Normally, they ran back to Marcus's condo, where he got ready while she caught the train to the office. Marcus had installed a shower in the restroom, so she would shower and dress there. She'd get started on organizing the notes she'd made during the run and Marcus would show up by nine thirty, looking as if he'd walked off a red carpet.

There was no showering together. Heck, there wasn't even any showering in the same building. That's how it worked.

But then, before ten minutes ago, there hadn't been any tears or hugs, either. Their physical contact was limited to handshakes and an occasional pat on the back and that was it.

"Shall I call him and reschedule?"

"Please do. Then we'll head back and I'll make a few calls." That was a perfectly normal set of Marcus responses.

Liberty was confident they were going to pretend that the touching and the holding and even the wedding date invitation had never happened. And that was fine with her, really.

But Marcus leaned forward. Even though he didn't touch her again, she still felt the air thin between them. His gaze dropped to her lips and, fool that she was, she still wanted that kiss that hadn't happened. The kiss that *couldn't* happen. "I promise you, Liberty—we won't lose that baby."

Three

It took Marcus the better part of three hours to find the right bureaucrat to deal with. The CEO of Children's Hospital, while sympathetic to Marcus's plight, could not legally provide any information on the baby. He did, however, call Marcus back in twenty minutes with the number of a DCFS supervisor.

The supervisor was less than helpful, but Marcus got the name of the manager of DCFS Guardians, who was responsible for assigning workers to these cases. It took some time to get ahold of the manager, and when he did, Marcus discovered a caseworker hadn't even been sent out.

"We're doing the best we can, Mr. Warren," the tired-sounding woman said. "But we have a limited amount of social workers and a limited amount of funds available to us. The baby will probably be in the hospital for several days. We'll send someone out as soon as we're able."

"That's not good enough," Marcus snapped.

"Well, how do you propose we deal with it?" the woman shot back.

The same way he dealt with everything. He wasn't about to let something like red tape get in his way. Marcus did a cursory web search and discovered that the current head of DCFS had gone to school with his father.

Well, hell. He should have started there. He knew how to play this game. He'd been raised playing an extended game of Who's Who. Political favors and donations were the kind of grease that made the wheels in Chicago run.

It took another twenty minutes to get through to the director's office and an additional twenty before Marcus had the man's personal promise that a caseworker would be assigned within the hour. "Of course, we don't normally keep nonfamily members updated..." the director said.

"I'd consider it a personal favor," Marcus said and in that, at least, he was being truthful.

Because after watching Liberty fold herself around that infant and cuddle the baby until he calmed down? After seeing Liberty's anguish as the baby was driven away in the ambulance? After impulsively pulling her into his arms because she was going to cry and feeling her body pressed against his?

After seeing that look of total gratitude when Marcus had said he'd take care of things?

Yeah, this was personal.

"Give your father my best," the man said at the end of the call.

"Will do!" Marcus said with false enthusiasm. He'd rather his father not find out about this particular conversation or the reason behind it. If Laurence and Marisa Warren knew about this, they'd give Marcus that disappointed look that, despite the decades of plastic surgery, was still immediately recognizable. It was one thing to trade political favors—but to do so for this? For an abandoned baby? Because his assistant got a little teary?

"What do you hope to gain out of this?" That's what his mother would say in her simpering voice, because that's what life was to her. Everything, every single human interaction, had a tally associated with it. You either gained something or you lost.

Warrens were never losers.

And his father? The man famous for his affairs with his secretaries? "If you want her, just take her." That's what his father would say.

He didn't want to be that man. He didn't want to use Liberty because he had all the power in their relationship. He was *not* his father.

Still, his father cast a long shadow. Marcus had gone to the university his parents had picked. His girlfriends had been preapproved daughters of their friends. Hell, even his company, Warren Capital, had been his father's idea. What better way to curry power and favor than to literally fund the businesses of tomorrow?

It had taken him years to loosen the ties that bound him to his parents, but he'd managed to separate his life from theirs. Liberty was a part of that, too. His mother had some friend of a friend she'd wanted him to hire—someone she could use to keep tabs on Marcus. Instead, he'd defied her by hiring a young woman from a family no one had ever heard of based on the strength of her recommendations and her insistence that she jogged regularly.

Marcus had paid for that act of defiance, just as he'd paid for refusing to marry Lillibeth Hanson. He may have lost favor with his parents, but he'd gained much more.

He'd gained his independence.

Still, he couldn't have his parents finding out about this. It simply wouldn't do for them to interest themselves in his life again.

"Mr. Warren?" Liberty stuck her head through his office door. He didn't miss the way that he was "Mr. Warren" again, as if she hadn't called him Marcus by the side of the jogging trail this morning.

"Yes?"

"Mr. Chabot is on the line." Marcus must have looked at her blankly, for she went on, "The producer for *Feeding Frenzy*? He wants to confirm the meeting when you're in Los Angeles after the wedding."

Right. Marcus had spent his entire morning tracking down someone—anyone—who knew about the little baby. He did actually have work to do.

"What did you tell him?"

She notched an eyebrow at him. "I put him on hold." The panic-stricken woman from the run this morning was gone and in her place was his competent, levelheaded assistant. Ms. Reese was impeccably dressed in a gray skirt suit with a rose-colored blouse underneath. Her hair was neatly pulled back into a slick bun and her makeup was understated, as always.

He'd wanted to kiss her this morning. The impulse had come out of nowhere. He'd watched her hold that child and felt her palpable grief when the ambulance had driven off. He'd wanted to hold her, to let her know it'd be okay. And then she'd looked up at him with her deep brown eyes and...

"Thank you, Ms. Reese," he said because what he needed right now was not to think about that impulse or how he'd joked that he should take her to the wedding only to realize he hadn't been joking. Which was a problem. She was an assistant—not part of his social circle. If he showed up with her, people would talk. Marcus Warren, slumming with his secretary. Or, worse, they'd assume that Liberty was manipulating him just as Lillibeth had.

But he wanted to take her. She was safe and trustworthy. And she was the one telling him to do what he wanted.

She gave him a little nod and turned to go.

"Liberty," he said.

She paused for a beat before she turned back around. "Yes?"

"I've made some calls about the baby. I'll let you know when I hear anything."

Her face softened and he was struck by how lovely she was. Underneath that executive-assistant mask was a beautiful woman. He just hadn't realized how beautiful until this morning. "Thank you."

He had nothing to gain by tracking down that baby. The child wouldn't bring him more power or money. The baby boy wouldn't be able to return a favor when Marcus wanted.

But he'd made a promise to Liberty.

He was going to keep it.

The ad mock-up for Rock City Watch drifted out of focus as Liberty wondered about that little baby. It'd been four days since she'd held him to her chest. Was he still in the hospital? Was he okay?

She shouldn't be this worried, she decided as she tried to refocus on the ad. Worrying wasn't going to help anything. And besides, Marcus had promised he'd look into it and she had to have faith that he'd keep that promise to her.

Of course it'd also been four days since Marcus had wrapped his strong arms around her and told her he'd find the baby because the child was important to her and she was important to Marcus.

Since that time, there'd been no hugs, no long looks. There'd been no more mention of the wedding, although that would have to change soon. If he continued to insist on going, he needed to pick a date. A safe date, she mentally corrected herself. Someone who wouldn't look at him and see nothing but a hot body and a huge...

Bank account.

The phone rang. "Warren Capital Investments. How may I assist you?"

"Ms. Reese." The coquettish voice of Mrs. Marisa Warren floated from the other end of the line. Liberty gritted her teeth. So this was how today was going to go, huh? "How is my son today?"

"Fine, Mrs. Warren." But Liberty offered no other information.

When she'd first been hired, Marcus had made it blisteringly clear that she worked for him, not for Laurence or Marisa Warren. If he ever caught her passing information to his parents about his business, his prospects or his personal life, well, she could pack her things and go. End of discussion.

Luckily, Liberty had gotten very good at telling people what they wanted to hear without giving anything away.

"I was wondering," Marisa simpered, "if my son has settled on a date for the Hanson wedding? It's a few weeks away and he knows how important it is."

When she'd first started fielding these nosy calls, Liberty hadn't entirely understood why Marcus was so determined that nothing of his life leak out to his parents. After all, she'd grown up dreaming of having a mother and a father who cared about her. And Marisa Warren seemed to care about her son quite a lot.

But appearances were deceiving. "Mrs. Warren," she said in her most deferential tone because it also hadn't taken her long to realize that while Marcus might treat her with respect and dignity, to his parents she was on approximately the same level as a maid. "I couldn't speak to his plans for the wedding."

"Surely you've heard something…"

Liberty focused on keeping her voice level. "As you know, Mr. Warren doesn't share personal information with me."

She wasn't sure at what point this wedding had crossed from personal to business and back again. When Marcus's relationship with Lillibeth had blown up in the media, she'd read what she could—but he'd never once broached the topic during office hours. It was only when they were running that he'd even touch on the subject—and even that was more about damage control than "feelings" and "sharing."

He'd asked her to prepare a roster of acceptable women with whom to attend this wedding. And then he'd asked her—however jokingly—to be his date.

"Hmph," Mrs. Warren said. It was the least dignified sound she was probably capable of making and, in her honeyed voice, it still sounded pretty. "Have him call me when he's free." She never asked to speak to Marcus when she called his office number. That was the thing that Liberty had realized about that first call. Mrs. Warren wasn't calling to talk *to* Marcus. She was calling to talk to Liberty *about* Marcus.

Liberty knew where her loyalty lay, even if Mrs. Warren didn't. "Of course, Mrs. Warren."

She hung up and finished analyzing the Rock City Watch ads. If Marcus was going to push them as a high-end luxury good, then the ads needed to be slicker. There was too much text talking about Detroit's revival, and the photography needed to give off a more exclusive vibe, she decided.

What rich people wanted was exclusivity. That's what she'd learned in the three years she'd worked in this office on North LaSalle. Not only did they want the best, they wanted to be damned sure that it was better than what everyone else had. It wasn't enough to own a great watch or a fancy car or live in an expensive building. Rich people wanted to make sure that theirs was the only one. She figured that was why they spent so much money on artworks. By definition, those were one of a kind.

This world was all still foreign to her, but after three years she felt as if at least she was becoming fluent in the language.

She was just finishing her notes when Marcus called out, "Ms. Reese?"

"Coming." She grabbed her tablet and the ad materials and walked into his office. This place, for example, was a perfect example of how a rich person simply had to have the very best. Even though Warren Capital was a relatively small operation—Marcus employed fifteen people to handle the finances and contracts—the business was located on LaSalle Drive on the top floor of one of the most expensive office buildings in Chicago. Marcus's office sat in the corner behind walls of glass that gave him expansive views of downtown and Lake Michigan. Warren Capital was the only company on this floor—no one else could claim this view. It was the best—and it was his.

And through sheer dint of will, Liberty managed to carve out a place where she could fit in this world. Sure, it was as an assistant and yes, she had to buy new running shoes every six months. It didn't matter. She loved this office, this view. Everything clean and bright. There were no holes in the wall, no critters scurrying about. If something broke, maintenance had it fixed within hours, if not minutes. The lights were always on and the heat always worked. This office was as far away from the apartment in the Cabrini-Green projects as she could get.

"Your mother called," she said, taking her usual seat in front of Marcus's desk. His office furniture reflected a modern sensibility—black leather seating, glass-topped desks of ebony wood and chrome. Even the art along the wall was modern. Among others, he had an Edward Hopper and a Mark Rothko—names she'd had to look up online because she certainly hadn't heard of them before. Marcus had bought the Rothko for $35 million.

Yes, he had one hell of an impressive…bank account.

"I assume to pump you for information about my wedding plans?" he asked without looking up.

"Correct. She's concerned about your date. Or lack thereof."

Marcus sighed heavily. "I've had an update on the baby, if you're still interested."

"What?" Her heart began to pound as he glanced at her in surprise. She tried again. "I mean, of course I'm still interested. Why wouldn't I be?"

"You hadn't asked."

She blinked at him. "You promised you'd make some calls. I didn't want to bother you."

He gave her a look that was partly amused. But she also thought she saw some of the tenderness beyond why he'd made that promise to her in the first place.

"Liberty," he said in a gentle voice. A creeping flush started at the base of her neck and worked its way down her back. Was it wrong to like how he said her name? Was it wrong to want him to say it some more? "You are not a bother to me."

She swallowed, willing her cheeks not to blush. They were getting off track. "What did you hear? About the baby?"

"Ah, yes." He looked down at his computer. The moment he looked away, Liberty exhaled.

"The baby has been discharged from the hospital."

She gasped. "How is he? Is he okay? Did they find his mother yet?"

"Apparently he's surprisingly healthy, given the circumstances—but no, they haven't located his parents yet." He gave her an apologetic look. "They don't seem to be looking too hard, despite my encouragement. I don't think they'll find the mother."

Liberty didn't know what to think because on one hand,

that poor child—being abandoned and never knowing his parents?

But on the other hand, he'd already been abandoned once. What if they found his mother—then what? There were other ways to abandon a child than just leaving him in a park. That she knew personally.

Marcus said, "I've been assured that the foster mother is one of their best and that the baby's needs will be met."

She gaped at him for a moment before she realized her mouth was still open. She got it shut and tried to remember to look professional. This was probably as good as the news would get. One of their best foster mothers? Personal assurances that the baby would be well cared for? Those were all things she'd never gotten when she was in the system. "That's wonderful. Can I visit him?"

Marcus looked at her in surprise, as if she'd asked for a space pony. "I didn't get the address."

"Oh." She stared down at her tablet. "I just thought…" She cleared her throat and tried to get back on track. "Here's the analysis of the Rock City Watch ad. I don't think it's hitting the target market you were looking for yet. And you still need to find a date for the wedding."

She stood and handed the ad material over to Marcus. Then she turned and headed for the door.

It was better this way. She'd done her part. Marcus had upheld his end of things. The baby was going to be fine.

Besides, what was she going to do? Adopt a child? Please. She worked from 7:00 a.m. until 6:00 p.m., five days a week, and she came in on Saturday to prepare for the next week's meetings. She had to. There was so much about his world that she didn't know and she couldn't afford to be exposed as an outsider, so she did her homework day in and day out.

She was at the threshold when Marcus spoke. "Liberty."

She paused. He wasn't going to ask her to the wedding again, was he? "Yes?"

She turned to face him. The way he was looking at her—it wasn't right. It wasn't normal anyway. What she would give for that look to be right because there was something to it, something that was possessive and intense. It scared her, how much she wanted him to look at her like that.

So she went on the defensive. "You can't want me to go to this wedding with you."

His lips curved into a seductive smile. "First off, aren't you the one telling me to do what I want?"

He couldn't mean that he really *wanted* to take her—could he? "Yes, but—"

He held up his hand like a king. "Do you want to see him again? The little boy."

She gave him a long, hard look. Was this a game? If so, she wasn't playing. "Mr. Warren, you're not going to make this awkward, are you? You'll get me the foster mother's address *if* I agree to attend this ridiculous wedding as your—what, your personal human shield?"

A muscle in his jaw twitched and he looked quite dangerous. Very few people said no to Marcus Warren. But she was one of them. "Just answer the question—do you want to see the baby again?"

She gritted her teeth. "Yes," she said, bracing for his counteroffer.

"That will be all," Marcus said, turning his attention back to his computer.

The dismissal was so sudden and unexpected that she just stood there for a moment. Marcus didn't look back up at her. He didn't acknowledge her continued presence at all. He merely ignored her.

It was not a good feeling.

Four

This time, the DCFS supervisor didn't hesitate to give Marcus the name and address of the foster home. All he had to do was say who he was and the woman practically fell over herself to give him what he wanted.

Well. It was nice that someone was acting appropriately. Because his executive assistant sure as hell wasn't.

Marcus stared at the information he'd written down on a piece of company letterhead. Hazel Jones. He googled the address and saw that it was way up in West Rogers Park.

This was ridiculous. He should be game-planning how to survive this wedding, not diverting his time, energy and accumulated favors for an abandoned baby and his assistant. And yet, here he was, doing just that.

There was nothing to be gained here. He did not need Liberty as a personal human shield and the implication—that he couldn't attend this stupid wedding without one—was an insult to his pride. He was a Warren, dammit all.

He didn't hide from anyone or anything and woe unto the person who tried to stand between him and his goal.

Who, at this exact moment, was Liberty Reese.

He strode out of his office to find Liberty on the phone. She glanced up at him, and the fact that he saw a hint of worry in her eyes only made him madder. What had he ever done to make her afraid of him? Not a damned thing. His father would have had her pinned to her desk by the end of her first month here and if she'd so much as sneezed wrong afterward, he would have done everything in his power to bury her.

And what had Marcus done? He'd treated her with respect. He'd never once laid a hand on her, never implied that her job was in some way connected to her sexuality.

All he had done was ask her to go to a wedding with him. And now she was treating him as if he was some lecherous old man to be feared.

"Yes," she said into the phone. "That's correct. No—no," she said in a more severe voice. "That is not the timetable. That information needs to be on my desk by the twelfth." She notched an eyebrow at him and mouthed "Yes?"

He crossed his arms and mouthed back, "I'll wait."

There it was again, that hint of worry. Okay, so maybe he shouldn't have asked her to the damned wedding. Hell, if he had his way, he wouldn't even be going to the thing.

"No, the twelfth. What part of that isn't clear? *The. Twelfth,*" Liberty snapped at the caller. Marcus grinned. He'd hired her because she was outside his parents' sphere of influence and she ran. But she'd turned into an exceedingly good assistant who was not afraid to push when she needed to.

She rolled her eyes at the phone and then dug through a small stack of papers on her desk, pulled one out and handed it to him.

"Available for the Hanson-Spears wedding" was the label of a column. Below was a list of names and phone numbers.

Marcus gave her a dull look, which she ignored. "Yes. Excellent. We look forward to seeing what you put together." She hung up the phone and took a deep breath. "I have to say that, at this point, the baby-wearables people are not winning any points in terms of organization or professionalism. They may not be ready to move to the next level."

Ah, yes. The company that wanted funding for a line of baby clothes and blankets with smart technology built into the fabric so anxious parents could monitor sleeping and eating habits from the comfort of their phones. The idea was intriguing, but he didn't like to see his money squandered by poor planning. "So noted."

She turned a bright smile to him. It was not real. "Was there something I could help you with?"

He held out the name and address he'd copied down. "Here. It's in West Rogers Park, up on the north side."

Liberty made a small noise, like a gasp she was trying her best to hold in. "I…" She looked up at him and at least for right now, any hint of worry or fake smiles was gone and he found himself looking down at the same woman whom he'd held in his arms beside the jogging path.

She would do anything for that baby, he realized. *Anything.* Even attend a wedding.

He knew it. And given the way her cheeks colored a pretty pink and she dropped her gaze, she knew it, too.

It'd make his life a hell of a lot easier. A plus-one for this wedding in exchange for a little information, and he wouldn't have to worry about finding a media-ready, parent-approved date who wouldn't view the event as a stepping-stone to bigger and better things. He could go with Liberty and might even enjoy himself. At the very least, they could run on the beach along the Pacific Ocean in the mornings instead of Lake Michigan.

She wouldn't be able to say no.

And he wouldn't be any better than his father was.

"As promised," he said and turned to walk back to his office.

He heard her chair squeak as she got up to follow him. "That's it?"

"That's it," he said, sitting down. He felt strange and he wasn't sure why. It wasn't a bad feeling. He stared at the list she'd given him. He'd gone out with a half dozen of these women and he knew the other half. Any one of these women would make a great date to this wedding and appease his mother.

He crumpled the paper up and threw it in the trash.

"You're not going to…" She let the sentence trail off but he could hear the words anyway. *You're not going to force the issue?*

"Insist you do something you obviously don't want to that falls outside of your job parameters? No," he replied, trying to sound casual. He was seriously just going to let this go? If he didn't get a date and he didn't take Liberty, he'd just go alone. Sure, his parents might disown him for it. "Why would I?"

He glanced at her then and wasn't surprised to see her looking as if she'd stepped into a room full of snapping alligators. "That's…thank you."

Even stranger, that made him feel better, as if her appreciation was all that he needed. "You're welcome."

But she didn't leave. Instead, she took another step into the office. "Marcus…"

It wasn't as if she hadn't said his name before. She had. But there was something about the way she said it this time that held him captive.

"I know I shouldn't ask this—but..." She looked down at the paper again as if he'd given her a sheet of solid gold. "Can I leave early today? Just today," she hurried to add. "This won't be a regular thing. I just..."

And he remembered how she'd soothed the baby, how she hadn't just hummed a lullaby but had told that little child that he was loved and he was strong and he could make it. And Marcus remembered how watching her holding that baby had rocked him to his core.

"I'll come in on Saturday and finish up whatever I don't get done this week," she offered, mistaking his silence for disapproval.

He stared at her. Did she think he didn't know she came in on Saturdays anyway?

Liberty went on. "This won't affect my job performance at all."

And he was reminded that he held all the power here and that meant he could gain something from this interaction.

He looked at his watch. It was three forty-five—early by their standards. "Here," he said, holding out his hand for the paper. "Give it to me."

"Oh." The disappointment on her face was a painful thing to see. "Yes, of course." She trudged forward—there was no other word for it—and handed over the paper. Then, without looking him in the eyes, she turned and headed back to her desk.

"Get your things packed up," he said, picking up his phone. He had nothing to gain from this but he was going to do it anyway. Because he wanted to. "We'll go together."

Somehow, Liberty found herself sitting in the passenger seat of Marcus's Aston Martin, zipping up Lake Shore Drive. One minute, she'd been crestfallen that she couldn't immediately go see the baby. The next, Marcus had been hustling her into his car—his very nice car—and personally driving her to the foster home.

She'd never been in his car before. Oh, sure, she'd attended a few business functions with him, but those were either after-hours events when she'd take the El as she always did or business lunches with potential clients when he'd have her order a car big enough for the entire group.

The Aston Martin was his personal car. And he drove it like a bat out of hell. Of course he did, she thought as she surreptitiously tried to grab on to the door handle when Marcus took the curve without braking. He drove as he ran.

"We don't have to go this fast," she said, trying to sound calm. "I'm not in that big of a hurry."

"This isn't fast," he replied and then, the moment they hit the straightaway, he gunned it. Liberty was pushed back into the seat as Marcus accelerated, weaving in and out of traffic. Lake Shore Drive was still mostly clear—it wouldn't fill up for another half hour with commuters. Marcus took full command of the road.

If she wasn't so concerned with dying in a fiery heap by the side of the road, she'd be forced to admit that it was kind of sexy. How often did a billionaire act as her personal chauffeur? Never.

They zipped up the drive in record time and then cut over on Peterson. There, at least, Marcus slowed down.

She was nervous. What if this foster home was one of the best—and it still wasn't very good? She tried to think back to the three homes she'd been in. The first home was fuzzy. It was just after she'd started kindergarten. Less than two weeks into the school year, her mom wasn't there when she got off the bus one day. Liberty had done okay on her own for a few days, going to see Grandma Devlin for food, but before long, she'd been in a foster home.

She didn't remember much, just that it got cold in her

room and that the other girls were mean to her. But she hadn't been hungry and there hadn't been the same kind of screaming and fights as at home.

"Why do you need to see him so badly?" Marcus asked when they got stuck at a light.

Liberty tensed. Were they still in the tug-of-war they'd been in earlier? Or were they back to normal? Since they were out of the office, was this the kind of conversation they might have while they were running?

Marcus glanced at her. "I'm just asking, Liberty," he said, sounding tired. "And it has nothing to do with the wedding."

Oh, if only she could *just* answer honestly. But how would that be possible? Because the truth hurt. And what would Marcus think if he knew the truth about addict moms and foster homes and being an unwanted, unloved little girl? Would he still want to take her to this stupid wedding—or would he look at her and see an imposter who was not to be trusted?

Still, she understood what he wanted to know. It wasn't her deepest, darkest secrets. It was a simple question that was only one step removed from polite conversation. She had to hope he'd be satisfied with her answer. "I had a little brother," she said and she was horrified to hear her voice quaver.

She'd never said those words out loud. Who would she have said them to when she was a kid? Her foster parents? They had enough kids to worry about. Her teachers? That would have only made them pity her more, and she had enough of that. Her friends? *Ha.*

"I didn't realize," Marcus replied. "I'm sorry."

"It's no big deal," she lied because that lie came as naturally to her as breathing air. None of it had been a big deal because she'd survived. She'd thrived. She could afford to ignore her past now.

Or she had been able to. Right until she'd seen the little baby in the trash. Then everything had come back.

She swallowed and tried to get her voice to work right again. "He was born with a lot of birth defects and didn't make it long." Which was a version of the truth that was palatable for Marcus's refined taste.

An uncomfortable silence boxed her in. She could see Marcus thinking and she couldn't have that because if he kept asking questions and she kept having to come up with better versions of the truth, sooner or later she'd either let the truth slip or be forced to tell a real lie. So she barged into the silence and said, "I appreciate you coming with me for this, but it wasn't necessary. You should be focusing on the list I gave you."

"You mean the list I threw away?" There—they were back to their early-morning teasing and banter.

"I have other copies," she announced and was rewarded with Marcus rolling his eyes and grinning at her. "You need to be focused on the wedding and the meeting with the producers, not on taking me to see an abandoned baby."

"Maybe this is what I want to do."

"Be serious, Marcus."

They hit another stoplight. "I am serious. You think you're the only one worried about that baby?"

She stared at him. "You are?"

"I can't explain it," he said in a quiet voice. "But watching you hold him…"

Oh. That was bad. The way his voice trailed off there at the end? The way he sounded all wistful and concerned?

Very, very bad. Damned bad, even.

She was not good for him. She could never be anything more than a valuable employee who got up too early every morning to jog with him. "I can't do anything for your reputation except drag it down."

Marcus didn't even look at her. He kept his attention on

the road, but she saw him clench his jaw again, just as he had in his office earlier. "My reputation isn't everything."

She desperately wanted to believe that, but she knew that in his world, her mere existence would be a scandal. "I'm not good for you," she said in a whisper.

He pulled onto a side street and parked. "I'll be the judge of that."

That was exactly what she was afraid of.

Five

Marcus got out of the car and looked around. He'd only ever lived in the Gold Coast, with luxury high-rises and doormen and valets. He rarely left the downtown area and when he did, it was to see the White Sox play or catch a Bulls or Blackhawks game at the United Center—from his owner's box, of course.

He looked up and down the street at the two-story buildings that stood side by side with older bungalows. Most yards were mowed. Was this a good neighborhood?

"This is nice," Liberty said, sounding shocked.

"What did you expect—slums?"

There was something about the way she avoided looking at him as she laughed that bothered him. She stared down at the address on the letterhead. He saw her hands were shaking.

"This one," she said, indicating a trim little bungalow. It was white with a wall of windows framed in dark wood.

The paint around the windows was a little chipped and the white was grubby, but it didn't look bad. He hoped.

"Ready?" he asked.

She took a deep breath and gave him an apologetic look. "You don't think this is ridiculous, do you?"

He had that urge to once again pull her into his arms and tell her it was all going to be fine. But he didn't. Instead, he told her, "Coming to see the baby? No. I want to do this with you."

Her eyes got huge again, but she didn't say anything. They walked up to the front door of the house and knocked. And waited. Marcus knocked again.

"She knows we're coming, right?" Liberty said. The panic in her voice was obvious. "Should we have—"

The door opened. "Mr. Warren?" Marcus almost grinned at the appearance of the little old lady standing before him. Maybe she wasn't that old, but she was petite, with a crown of white hair cut into a bob and a huge pair of vintage-looking glasses on her nose.

"Mrs. Jones, hello. We spoke on the phone." He offered his hand but she just nodded and smiled. "This is Liberty Reese. We found the child together and we just wanted to see how he's doing."

"It's a pleasure to meet you, Mrs. Jones," Liberty said. She sounded stiff.

"How sweet of you to come. Please, call me Hazel. All my friends do. Come in, come in. Shut the door behind you, if you don't mind." She turned and began to climb up a short flight of stairs.

Marcus made sure to shut the front door behind him, which took a little shove. The entryway contained another set of doors that led both upstairs and downstairs, and he had to wonder if this was a single-family home or if someone else lived in the basement.

Hazel and Liberty finally went through the upstairs door and Marcus followed, shutting it behind him. Then he looked around.

Wow. Once, when he'd been really little, he'd had a nanny who loved *The Brady Bunch*. His parents didn't believe in television, so getting to watch any show was a big deal to him. The nanny—Miss Judy—let him catch a show if he got all his lessons done. She'd make a bowl of popcorn and they'd snuggle on the couch and for a half hour at a time, he'd gotten a glimpse at what normal might look like.

It'd been years since he'd thought of *The Brady Bunch*. But this was like walking into the Brady house. Everything looked as if it was original to the 1960s or '70s—the pine paneling, the vinyl covers over the sofa cushions, the preponderance of autumn gold and orange everywhere. Marcus leaned over to catch a glimpse through a doorway—yes, there were avocado-green appliances in the kitchen.

This was one of the best foster homes in the system?

"He's in the nursery," Hazel was saying. "He's still napping. Oh, they sleep so much the first week or so, but he's starting to wake up."

"Is he okay?" Liberty asked anxiously.

"I think he's perfect," Hazel said as she guided them through a small dining room and past two doorways that led to a bedroom and a television room. The third doorway was the nursery. "I understand your concerns, though. I've had children who were coming off drugs or the like and he doesn't seem to have those problems." She stopped and sighed. "His poor mother. One has to wonder."

"Yes," Liberty said. "One does."

Hazel gave Liberty a maternal smile as she patted her arm. "It's good you've come. This way."

They all crowded into the small room. A metal crib was by one wall and a larger, wooden crib up against another.

There was a dresser with a blue terry-cloth pad on it next to a worn rocking chair. Marcus had to wonder how long Hazel Jones had had these things—since her own children had been babies?

All over two of the walls were pictures of babies, he realized. Old pictures, with the edges curling and the colors faded to a gold and brown that matched the furniture in the rest of the house. There were hundreds of pictures of little babies all over the place.

Next to a window was an antique-looking swinging chair that squeaked gently with every swing. And inside the swing was the baby boy. He was clean and dressed and Marcus swore he'd grown in the past five days, but there was no mistaking that child. Marcus would know him anywhere. How odd, he thought dimly.

Liberty made a noise that was half choking, half gasping. "Oh—oh," she said, covering her mouth.

Hazel patted her on the arm again. "You're his guardian angels, you and your boyfriend. He would have likely died if it hadn't been for you."

"We're not—" Liberty started to say, but Hazel cut her off.

"It'll be time for his bottle in a few. Would you like to feed him?"

"Could I?" Liberty turned to Marcus, her brown eyes huge. "Do we have time?"

As if she had to get his permission. "Of course."

"I'll be right back." In contrast to her slow climb up the stairs, Hazel moved quickly to the kitchen. "Don't go anywhere!" she jokingly called out.

"Is this what you wanted?" Marcus asked Liberty as they stared at the baby.

"Oh, God, yes. He's okay," she said as if she still couldn't believe it. The baby exhaled heavily and turned his head away from the window. Liberty gasped and flung out a hand in his direction and Marcus took it. He gave her a squeeze of support and she squeezed back. "Look at him," she said in awe.

"Is this place okay for him, do you think?" Marcus looked around the room again at the worn, battered furniture. "They said it was one of their best homes…"

"No, it's really lovely." Marcus stared down at her, but she was still looking at the baby. "And it seems like she only has him right now. This is *amazing*."

There was something in the way she said it, the way she *meant* it, that struck him as odd. But before he could ask about it, Hazel said brightly, "Here we are."

He dropped Liberty's hand and stepped out of the way. Hazel handed him a bottle and he took it, even though he had no idea how to feed a baby.

"Does he have a name yet?" Liberty asked Hazel.

"Oh, no. He's still Baby Boy Doe." As if on cue, the baby began to lift his little hands and scrunch up his eyes. "I suppose he should have a name, shouldn't he?"

"William," Liberty said without hesitation. "He's William." She said it with such conviction that again, Marcus found himself staring at her.

"Oh, that's lovely. My husband was Bill. That's a good name." The baby began to fuss and Hazel deftly carried him over to the dresser and laid him out on the pad. She unzipped his blanket-thing—a blanket with arms? Was there a name for that? Hazel began to change his diaper with the kind of practiced motion that made it clear she could do this in the dark, in her sleep. Marcus wondered how many babies she'd changed just like that.

"We never had children," Hazel went on as she got out a clean diaper from the top drawer, all the while never taking her hand off the baby's belly. "But I loved babies so… I was offered an early retirement from my teaching position back in 1988 and I decided that I was going to be a grandmother one way or another."

"All babies?" Liberty asked.

"Oh, yes. I just love this age. They're such little angels. I can't keep up with them when they start crawling and walking, though." Hazel shook her head. "Babies are just my speed."

Marcus watched as Hazel changed the diaper. She made it seem easy but the mostly naked infant was squirming and then there was the cleaning part and…

Suddenly, he was terrified. It wasn't the same kind of terror he'd felt when he'd opened the box and found this child—that had been stark panic, with a life hanging in the balance. That danger was safely past, thank God. But when Hazel got the diaper on and asked Liberty if she wanted to help re-dress William, and Liberty still looked as if she might start sobbing with relief at any moment, the whole scene was so far outside his realm of experience that he might as well have landed on Mars.

Liberty got his tiny little feet back into the blanket contraption and zipped him up. "Here we go," Hazel said in a singsong voice as she picked William up. "Dear, why don't you sit in the rocker?"

Liberty sat and Hazel laid the baby in her arms. In that moment, everything about Liberty changed; it was as if he were looking at a different woman. This wasn't his take-charge assistant—this was Liberty, the real woman.

Hazel took the bottle from Marcus and showed Liberty how to hold it. The older woman got a little pillow that had been next to the rocking chair and used that to prop Liberty's arms up. "There we go. He's been eating quite a bit, poor dear." For the first time in a while, she seemed to notice Marcus. "Oh—would you like a chair?"

"I'm fine," he insisted. He couldn't take his eyes off Liberty and William. There was something about them—something he'd seen that first time in the park…

"You're amazing with him," he told Liberty and he meant it. Yeah, he'd found the child, but it was Liberty who'd cooled him down and got him to stop crying. It was because of Liberty that Marcus had used his clout to make sure the baby got into the best home.

It was Liberty who'd named him.

Then she looked up at him and smiled and everything that Marcus knew to be true about himself was suddenly… not true. Not anymore.

He was Marcus Warren. A trust-fund billionaire, gossip column fodder and a potential reality-television star. He had a business and a reputation to manage. He had to carry on the Warren family name.

And quite unexpectedly, none of it mattered. What mattered was seeing Liberty rock that tiny baby and smile at him with that silly joy on her face, as if she'd been waiting her whole life for this exact moment.

What mattered was knowing he'd made this moment happen. Because he wanted that silly joy on her face. He wanted to be the one who made her smile, who gave her everything her heart desired. Not because it would give him leverage, but because it made her happy.

His entire life had been about accumulation. Things, power, favors—more and more and more. Never enough.

What if…

William's mouth popped off the bottle and he squirmed. "Oh, is he okay?" Liberty asked Hazel.

The two of them fussed over the baby and Liberty got him burped. Then Hazel took William back and turned to Marcus. "Would you like to hold him?"

"Sure," he said, sitting in the rocking chair. Liberty

propped the pillow under his arm. He tried to position his arms the way she had.

She looked down at him skeptically. "Have you ever held a baby before?"

His face got hot. "No?"

Liberty sighed, but at least she was grinning as she moved his hands into approximately the right position as if it was no big deal to physically rearrange him. But it only made that nearly out-of-body experience he was having that much worse.

What if...

"Here we are," Hazel said, handing William to Marcus. The baby sighed and scrunched up his nose.

Marcus was dimly aware that Hazel and Liberty were still talking, but he didn't really hear them. Instead, he stared down at the child in his arms.

William was so small—how was this human going to grow up and be a regular-sized person? "Hi, William," Marcus whispered as the baby waved one of his hands jerkily through the air.

Without thinking about it, Marcus shifted and held one of his fingers up against William's hand. The baby grabbed on at the same time his little eyes opened up all the way, and in that moment Marcus was lost. How could anyone have walked away from this baby? This must have been what Liberty had felt when she'd held the baby in the park.

They couldn't lose this baby. He'd thought he'd done his part, getting William into one of the best foster homes— but now that Marcus had seen Liberty with him, now that he'd held William himself, how could he walk away from this child?

He looked around the room again. Hazel was a good foster mother for a baby, he decided. But the stuff she had to work with was ancient. Marcus eyed the baby swing William had been in when they got here. The thing looked like a death-trap of metal and plastic.

His phone buzzed in his pocket, which startled the baby. William began to fuss and Hazel swooped in and plucked him from Marcus's arms. "There, now," she soothed.

"Sorry," Marcus said as he dug out his phone. The missed call had been from his mother. This couldn't be good. It was already past five.

"We should go," Liberty said. "Hazel, thank you so much for letting us visit William. This was wonderful. I'm so glad he's got you."

With William tucked against her chest, Hazel waved the compliment away. "You're more than welcome to come back. Just give me a call!"

"Could we?" Liberty glanced at Marcus, her cheeks coloring brightly. "I mean, I'll do that."

"We can come back," he agreed. And he wasn't just saying that—he really did want to see the baby again. More than that, he wanted to see Liberty with the baby again.

Liberty gave him another one of her shy smiles, as if she'd been hoping he'd say that but hadn't dared to ask.

As they walked toward the front door, Hazel followed them. "You two should consider applying for adoption," she said. "A nice couple like you? And because you found him, you might have a better chance of getting him. If they don't find his birth mother, that is," she added, sounding sad. "Poor dear."

Liberty jolted. "I don't—"

"We'll discuss it," Marcus said. He put his hand on Liberty's back and guided her down the stairs. "Thanks so much."

He made sure to shut the door behind them.

Six

Liberty stood on the sidewalk in a state of shock. She knew she needed to pull herself together but she was weirdly numb right now.

"That place was a time warp," Marcus said, stepping around her to the car and opening the passenger door for her.

She blinked at him. Hazel was a warm, loving, capable woman who had only one child in her charge and, by all appearances, would dote on William as if he were her own. That was weird enough, but now? Marcus Warren was opening her door for her. In what world did *any* of this make sense?

"Liberty?" Then he was touching her again, his hand in the small of her back as he gently propelled her toward his waiting car as if he was her chauffeur instead of her billionaire boss. Warmth flowed up her back from where he touched her and she wanted nothing more than to lean into him. "Are you all right?"

No. No, she wasn't. Everything had changed and she

didn't know how she'd ever be the same again. But she had to try. "I can't—you don't have to come back."

Marcus snorted in amusement. "I never have to do something I don't want," he said. "You were right. We can't lose him."

"We?" That word sounded different in her ears now, foreign almost. There was no "we" where Marcus and she were concerned. Not outside the office or off the jogging path. Or beyond her carefully guarded fantasies. "But…"

"Come on," he said, almost pushing her into the car. "Let's get some dinner. We can talk then."

"Dinner?" She couldn't make sense of anything he was saying. *We. Dinner.* "No—wait," she said when he got into the driver's seat. "You don't have to take me to dinner. You should be taking a potential wedding date—not me."

"Maybe I am taking a potential date to dinner."

And they were right back to where they'd been earlier. Well, this time she was not going to mess around. The sooner he realized how radically inappropriate she'd be as a wedding date, the sooner they could get back to their regularly scheduled programming. "Marcus, I'm *not* going. I'm not good enough for you, for that crowd. I know it. Everyone else there will know it. You're the only one who doesn't seem to realize it."

"That's not—"

She cut him off because he had to see reason. She didn't know how much longer she could be this strong. "That's not all. Why would I want to go to this wedding? Why would I want to watch Lillibeth hurt you again? Because you know she's going to try. And everyone will be watching to see how bad it's going to be. You'll be back in the media again. And I don't want to be a part of that. I don't want to be another reason people try to tear you down. I care too much about you to let that happen."

The last part just slipped out. She hadn't meant to say that she cared about him at all, but she'd built up a head of steam. But it was the truth—a truth that she couldn't bury anymore.

"Liberty," he said. And then something horrible and wonderful happened—Marcus touched her. He cupped her face in the palm of his hand.

"I just don't want you to be hurt again," she breathed. And even though she knew she shouldn't, she reached up and held his palm against her skin.

"You won't hurt me. I know you too well for that."

There it was again, that blind trust he had in her. And she knew—*knew*—that if he learned the truth, the whole truth and nothing but the truth about her junkie mom and her unknown father, he would be hurt.

She wanted to lean into his touch, but she couldn't because she was already starting to slip up and if she let herself get swept away in his touch, in his longing looks, something even more damaging might come out of her mouth.

So she shook him off. "If you don't want to, don't. Don't go to the wedding. Don't do the reality show. You said it yourself—your reputation isn't everything. You don't need to do any of that stuff. Do what *you* want."

He stared at her for a moment, but she refused to make eye contact because she didn't know if she could handle it. One searing look from Marcus Warren might break her resolve. So she kept her gaze locked on the windshield.

He started the car and began to drive without answering.

"Please take me back to the office. I'll finish the work I didn't get done earlier."

"Don't worry about it," he said. He sounded distant.

She fought the urge to apologize, to backpedal—to take it all back. She wanted to go back to the way things had been a week ago, when he'd tease her during the run and she earned his respect by being invaluable to his business, when she didn't offer opinions on his personal life and she didn't run the risk of letting the facts of her life slip out at every turn.

But then, that'd mean not finding William—not knowing that he was alive and healthy and cared for. And she couldn't imagine that. She'd seen that baby for a total of an hour and a half and she couldn't imagine life without him.

You two should consider applying for adoption. Liberty would be lying to herself if Hazel's idea didn't sound like a dream come true. She'd long fantasized about Marcus. He was gorgeous, one of the richest men in the city, and she liked him. She hated running but she liked running with him. She liked his jokes and how he treated her and how he'd put that shower in the ladies' room so she could change without going all the way back to her apartment in Logan Square.

And she'd liked the way he looked holding that baby and smiling down at him as if he really did care. It hadn't mattered that he'd had on a suit that probably cost thousands or that William was one burp away from ruining that suit. Marcus had smiled and cooed and held his hand anyway. William was important to Marcus because William was important to her.

She'd spent her entire adolescence and adulthood trying so hard to overcome her abandonment. Her life was built around making sure no one could forget about her again. She worked harder than anyone else. She never stopped working. In college, she'd held down two jobs and carried a full class load and never done anything fun like party or date. Never. She'd passed as white because she could and because it meant she was that much further away from Jackie Reese's life, because passing meant that she had to work only twice as hard to get ahead, not four times as hard.

What if Marcus learned the truth about her? About her mother's criminal history and overdose death? About Liberty's time in foster homes? About how she wasn't really who she said she was?

Would he still look at her and smile as he'd smiled at William? Or would he look at her and see who she really was—a hooker's daughter who lied her way into a better life?

"We're here," he said, startling her out of her thoughts.

She looked up to see that, instead of pulling up to the office, they were in front of a restaurant. A valet in a red jacket opened her door. "Welcome to Alinea."

She turned to Marcus. "Wait, what?"

"Dinner," he said in his nonnegotiable voice.

"Marcus! We can't do this!"

Unexpectedly, he leaned over, his face very close to hers. "We can't? Why can't we?"

"I'm your assistant. You're my boss. I'm not…"

"Don't you dare say you're not good enough for me, Liberty, because it's not true."

Her heart began to pound. He really meant that. Worse, he believed it. He couldn't imagine that she was anything other than what she was. If he knew…

But when he said things like that, she wanted to tell him. She wanted to say yes, that she'd go with him—anywhere with him.

But her reality trumped any fantasy she had. Marcus simply couldn't know the truth. She clung to the only thing she could—their professional relationship. "But I work for you."

He lifted an eyebrow, which made him look like a fox. She felt like a hen, that much was for sure. "I could fix that."

She gasped. "Is that…are you *threatening* me?" She needed this job. She *was* this job. Getting another would mean risking exposure all over again. References would be checked. Questions would be asked. Judgments would be made.

SARAH M. ANDERSON 63

He looked hurt by this. "No—of course not. It's just..."
He sighed heavily. "Look, it's been a long day. I'm hungry.
You're hungry. I want dinner. This isn't a date, okay? We'll
talk business."

"You won't ask me about the wedding again?"

"I won't ask," he promised.

Marcus settled into the booth and watched as Liberty
hesitated before sliding in opposite him. The maître d' said,
"Mr. Warren, the wine list."

"Thank you, Winston."

When Winston had departed, Liberty whispered, "You
come here often?"

Marcus shrugged. "Enough that they have a table waiting for me. I enjoy dining out."

"So," she said in a too-bright voice. "Business."

"Yes," he agreed, staring at the menu. "But first, dinner."

Liberty frowned at the menu. "What's good? I don't
even..." Her voice trailed off. "What's haricots verts?"

"Green beans in French," Marcus said with a grin.

"Why don't they just say green beans?"

Marcus snorted. "Like commoners? Please."

Liberty gave him a nervous little smile and he remembered one of her excuses for why she wouldn't go to the wedding with him—because she wasn't good enough.

"What's a foam? A truffle-oil foam? Is that even food?"

"It's more of a taste—a flavor on the palate," he told her.
"This isn't the first time you've eaten in a restaurant like
this, is it? We've gone to lunches in similar places."

She didn't look him in the eyes. "We've never been here.
I'd remember it." As she said it, a waiter walked past with
a balloon. He deposited it at a nearby table and the diners
popped the balloon and started eating it.

Liberty blanched. "I'd definitely remember *that*. Are they…"

"It's a house specialty." This was wrong, all wrong. At the time, he'd just wanted a nice meal with her, and Alinea was one of the nicest restaurants in the country, with prices to match. "What do you order when we dine out?" He felt bad that he didn't remember. True, when they ate together at a restaurant, he was entertaining clients, but that suddenly seemed like the sort of thing he should know about her.

She blushed. "I usually either order what you order or I order the special."

Why hadn't he ever noticed that before? "But what if you don't like what I order?"

"I'm not picky." She kept staring at the menu as if it were written in, well, a foreign language.

He plucked it from her hands. "What are you in the mood for? Steak? They have a lobster dish that's amazing."

She stared at him as if he, too, had started speaking in tongues. "There was steak on that menu?"

He grinned as the waiter came back. "I'll have the lobster plate and the lily bulbs. The lady will have the *wagyu* plate and the fourteen textures."

"Excellent choices," the waiter said. "May I recommend a 2000 Leflaive Bâtard white burgundy with that?"

"Is that the Montrachet Grand Cru?"

The waiter bowed in appreciation. "It is."

"That'll do."

"If I may be so bold," the waiter said, "we have the pâté sucrée tonight."

"That sounds fine," Marcus said, handing over the menus. He looked to Liberty. "Unless you wanted to try the balloons? They're quite fun. Apple flavored, right?" The waiter nodded again.

Liberty goggled at him. "No, what you ordered is fine."

In other words, she had no idea what he'd ordered. He made a mental note that the next time he took her out to dinner to pick some place more accessible—a nice steak house or something.

"Do I even want to know how much this is going to cost?"

Marcus waved this question away. "It's not important."

"What do you mean, it's not important? Of course it's important. I can't expect you to pay for my dinner."

That made him smile. "Did you think we were going Dutch here?"

"This isn't a business lunch, Marcus. You can't expect me to—"

Actually, he was rapidly losing his grip on what, exactly, he could expect from her. "Liberty, stop, for heaven's sake. That bottle of wine alone probably costs five or six hundred dollars."

All the blood drained out of her face. "And that's not important?"

He knew she was serious but… "What's a six-hundred-dollar bottle of wine to me?"

She still looked like a ghostly copy of herself. "I just—six hundred dollars? When I was growing up…" She stumbled over her words and went silent.

He went on. "Liberty, when you're a billionaire, at a certain point, money loses all meaning. If it were a six-million-dollar bottle of wine, well, it still wouldn't make a big impact in the long run."

He was not making things better, that much he could tell. She looked as if he'd stabbed her with the business end of a wine bottle. "You—you really mean that, don't you?"

"Money is like air. I don't think about it. I don't have to do anything to make more of it suddenly appear. It just *is*." She stared at him, openmouthed. "I understand that most people don't live like that—I'm not a complete idiot," he hurried to add, which did not necessarily improve things. "There's no way I'd expect you to foot part of the bill in a place like this."

He took her in—the pale face, the eyes and mouth wide with shock—and wondered about her life. She'd always been this smartly dressed, exceptionally prepared young woman. Sure, he knew the suits weren't Chanel or Armani, but she'd fit his image of a middle-class woman working her way up.

But was she?

"So," she said nervously. "Thank you for dinner. Whatever it's going to be."

"You're welcome." There was a pause, as if she didn't know what to say next. Frankly, he wasn't that sure, either. "So. We're not talking about the wine."

She gave him a baleful look. For some reason, it made him grin. "No. And we're not talking about the wedding."

"No." He considered. "Are we talking about William?" Because he had some questions for her. And they weren't necessarily fact-finding questions, per se. He had a flood of confused emotions that he hadn't anticipated and didn't know how to process. Tender emotions. It was…odd. He needed to make sense of what he was feeling and he wanted to know if Liberty was feeling the same way.

There it was again, that shy little smile. "I thought we were going to discuss business."

"Fine. Business." He thought back to something that had come up earlier. "Why do you work every Saturday?"

The question clearly caught her off guard. "What? I don't—I mean—you know about that?"

"Of course," he said. "There's very little that goes on in my company that I'm not aware of."

Her cheeks reddened as she stared at the top of the table. "I'm just trying to get a jump on the week." But there was something about the way she said it that didn't sit quite right. Then she looked up at him and gave him a sly smile. "I have this boss, you see—he appreciates an assistant who knows as much as she can about potential clients, market conditions and so on."

"Sounds like a real bastard," he agreed. "But every Saturday?"

She shrugged, as if that were no big deal.

There was something about this he didn't like, but he was having trouble putting his finger on it, which meant he liked it even less. "I don't pay you to work six days a week."

"You pay me a lot," she said and then added, "It's a very generous salary. I don't mind."

"But don't you have a life?" It came out before he realized what he was saying, but there was no taking it back.

Liberty's eyes narrowed as she drew herself up and squared her shoulders.

"I mean," he quickly backtracked, "even I don't spend that much time in the office and it's my business. It's not healthy. You've got to make time to have a social life and—I don't know, go grocery shopping or something."

He did some quick calculations. They ran five mornings in a row and she was basically putting in an extra workday. "You're working sixty-hour weeks, every week. I pay you for forty hours."

"You pay me to do a job. This is what it takes to do the job well," she countered, looking trapped. "And for the record, I have a life. I buy groceries. I shop. I watch television."

"Do you have a social life? Spend time with your family? Do you date?"

Her eyes flared. "Not that it's any of your business."

Maybe it wasn't. He didn't know why he'd asked about her dating, except that he wanted to know. "Here's what I don't understand," he went on. "When I first realized you were working weekends, I thought it was because you were trying to get ahead—which made sense. You'd put in the hours and prove yourself to be invaluable—which you are," he hurried to add because this seemed like a good place for a compliment. "People who work like you do have a plan. They have goals. They stay in a job for a year or two, learn everything they can, and then they move on. They take the next job that can challenge their skill set, the next job that can lay the groundwork for the job after that—they network, build up references, the whole nine yards. They climb a ladder. Yet it's been three years and you're still here with me, fending off my mother and scolding inventors who can't get their shit together. Why?"

"I like this job. It's a good job."

He scoffed at this. "It's not like there's one good job in the world and this is it. What about the time Jenner tried to poach you? He offered to make you his assistant—at, I believe, almost double the salary. And you didn't take it."

Erik Jenner was an old friend of his, going back to prep school. They played golf and talked sports and tried to outdo each other with bigger boats, better cars and everything else. It hadn't surprised him at all that Jenner had tried to poach Liberty for his real estate business. He was surrounding himself with the best talent money could buy.

What had surprised him was that Liberty had said no. Not that she'd told Marcus—Jenner himself had related this whole story with the air of one who had failed in his quest and didn't know why.

Marcus didn't, either.

"I didn't like Mr. Jenner," she countered. That got Marcus's attention. Then she quickly added, "I mean, I didn't like his business model. His real estate developments seemed unsustainable."

"You play it safe, Liberty. You're more than smart enough to go elsewhere and move up the ladder. But you won't take the risk. Are you really content to be my executive assistant for the rest of your life?"

She opened her mouth to answer, but just then their first courses arrived. The waiter explained their dishes for them and instructed Liberty on how to eat hers. She gamely sampled her dish while giving Marcus's lily bulbs the side eye.

"They're good," he told her, spearing one on his fork. "Try one."

He held out his fork to her and, after a moment's pause, she leaned forward. Her lips closed over the bulb and he suddenly realized exactly why he'd asked if she was dating anyone—it wasn't because he was concerned that she was burning herself out.

It was because watching her lips slide off the tines of his fork was close to a holy experience. Her eyes widened as she chewed and then the tip of her tongue slipped out and traced the seam of her lips.

"I don't know how you can accuse me of playing it safe," she said in a low voice, "when you're feeding me bulbs and God only knows what else." She dipped her spoon into her bowl and held it out for him to taste. "I take *lots* of risks."

Seven

Marcus leaned forward, with a glint in his eyes that she wasn't sure she'd ever seen before. "Do you?" he asked, and then took her spoon into his mouth.

Liberty's heart beat so fast that she wouldn't be surprised if Marcus could see it thumping in her chest. Him feeding her? Her feeding him? She stared at his mouth, at his lips. Was it wrong to wonder what it'd be like to feel his lips moving on her body as they moved on her spoon?

Would it be bad if she found out?

She shook her head. That must be the wine talking because right now? This was a hell of a risk. The kind that could put her job in jeopardy. Under any normal circumstances, it would be unacceptable.

But there was very little about today that felt normal. Including this dinner.

Especially this dinner.

Still, she didn't know how to answer him. So instead

she turned her attention back to her dish. She was forced to call it a dish because she simply had no other words to describe it. She wasn't sure that what she was eating qualified as food.

She took a sip of the most expensive wine she'd ever had. "This is good. Weird, but good."

"Next time, we'll go to a steak house," he told her in between bulbs.

"Next time?" Because this dinner walked a fine line between a business dinner and a date. Having more of the same would be decidedly date-like.

She couldn't date Marcus, no matter how wonderful it might be. She wasn't the kind of woman who belonged in a place like this, drinking wine that cost hundreds of dollars and eating things that barely met the basic standards of being edible while also probably costing several hundred dollars. There hadn't been any prices on the menu, which, in her experience, was a bad sign.

She was the kind of woman who considered a five-dollar bottle of wine and a carryout pizza to be a rare treat. If she got really wild, she'd go to the small Thai restaurant a block away and get *pad see ew*.

"The question remains," Marcus said, finishing his bulbs. "You haven't left me. Why?"

"Because." She was aware that wasn't much of an answer. But it was the only answer she had.

Because Marcus was right. She'd worked her ass off to get this position, to get to a point in her life where she wasn't living on the line that divided poverty and extreme poverty. The fact that she'd made it this far? Gotten off public assistance, paid off all her college debt and was finally able to say that she was comfortable? *Valuable?*

Why on God's green earth would she want to risk that?

"*Because* is not an answer," Marcus said. The waiter reappeared, cleared their dishes and refilled their wineglasses. Liberty sipped—slowly.

You haven't left me. That was what he'd asked and she'd truly never thought of it in that light. She'd stayed with a job. She hadn't stayed with the man.

Had she?

She thought back to Erik Jenner, how he'd arrived in the office unexpectedly one day. He'd propped himself up on the corner of her desk and smiled down at her. It wasn't the kind of smile that Marcus gave her—no, this was different. Jenner was attractive and rich—on paper, he wasn't that different from Marcus. But the way he'd looked at her made her uncomfortable.

He'd offered her a lot of money and a lot of responsibility if she'd jump ship. And she'd be lying if she said the money wasn't tempting.

But she hadn't wanted to risk it—any of it. Having a boss who made her uncomfortable. Starting over in a place where people would ask questions about her: where she'd gone to school, who her family was. As tempting as the money had been, it hadn't made up for the stability—the safety—that Marcus offered her.

"I don't want you to work on Saturdays anymore," Marcus announced over the lip of his wineglass.

"It would affect my job performance," she informed him.

"Fine. Then I'm giving you a raise. I pay you now for a forty-hour week. I'll up that by twenty percent."

She choked on her wine. "You'll *what*?"

Oh, that lazy smile—that could be her undoing, if she let it. She wouldn't let it. "Really, Liberty, you need to work on your negotiation skills. A good negotiator would have come back with thirty percent."

"I wasn't even asking for a raise!"

"True. A good negotiator would have used Jenner's job

offer to ask for one. He offered you thirty percent more than I'm paying you with stock options. The benefits package was considerable and you didn't even tell me about it." He wagged a finger at her as if he were scolding her. "I've seen you be a hard-ass with clients for me. Can't you do that for yourself?"

"I don't—" She exhaled.

"Ask me for something," he demanded, leaning forward and pinning her with his gaze. "Right now. Tell me what you want."

Liberty began to panic because she'd had enough wine that she couldn't be 100 percent sure that she wouldn't say something horrible, such as she wanted him. Because she did. This felt like a dream: Marcus Warren sitting across from her in a dimly lit restaurant, offering her what her heart desired. All she had to do was say the word.

She bit down on the inside of her cheek—hard. The pain snapped her out of her reverie. "I want my food," she said in a light tone. "I think your bulb thingies were better than my—my whatever it was."

He stared at her. "Are you afraid of me? Is that it?"

"Don't be ridiculous," she retorted.

"Then why won't you tell me what you want? Come on, Liberty! Do you realize that today, asking if you could leave early to go see William—that was the first time you've *ever* asked to leave work early? That's not normal. People have appointments, stuff comes up. People get sick. But not you."

"Did it ever occur to you that I already have everything I want? I like my job. I like working for you. Nothing has to change."

He gave her a look then that seared her. Heat flushed her, starting low in her back and racing upward like a forest fire. He leaned forward and although she knew she needed to lean back, to break his gaze—to do anything to put a little distance between them—she felt the pull of his body on hers. He was like gravity. That's what this was—an unseen force that guided her every movement.

"What if it's already changed?" He reached out and put his hand on top of hers. His touch was warm against her skin—intimate, even. The air around them felt charged with electricity, and the shock of it all made it hard to sit still. "What if we can't go back?"

The waiter arrived with their dishes and Liberty pulled her hand away and put it in her lap. Marcus had forgotten what he'd ordered, but he didn't care. Liberty stared at her food with open distrust—he couldn't blame her. Her *wagyu* steak looked like charcoal briquettes, complete with embers. The waiter went through the premeal instructions again but Marcus wasn't listening.

What if everything had already changed?

There was no what-if here. Everything *had* changed. Nothing had been the same between them since the moment he'd found that little baby boy and watched Liberty clutch him to her chest. In that moment, he'd seen her differently. She'd been more than his employee then—much more.

Liberty gamely poked at her steak dish. "This is food, right?"

"Eat slowly. The experience is almost as important as the food," he told her, looking at his own plate. Ah, yes—he remembered now. The lobster.

"Eating quickly could be deadly," she quipped as she blew out a smoking ember on her beef.

Why wouldn't she tell him one thing she wanted? Why wouldn't she demand a raise, more perks—anything of him?

I care too much about you. That's what she'd said in the car and that was another moment they couldn't back away from.

He watched her pick at her food. "This is good," she said, diligently forging ahead as if, in fact, nothing had changed.

"I'm glad," he said casually. What if these things were connected? The fact that she cared for him and the fact that she never asked anything of him? Except when it came to William.

Because she cared for that little baby, too.

"What are we going to do about William?" he asked, trying to keep his tone light.

Not that it worked. She paused, her fork halfway to her mouth. He had the urge to lean over and kiss her, but he was pretty sure he'd get a steak knife to the palm if he did that. "We?"

"Yes, we. We're in this together. When do you want to go see him again?"

She took her time answering and he worked on his lobster. Not that he tasted much of it. He was too busy watching her. "I was unaware there was a *we* where William was concerned."

"Of course there's a *we*. We found him. We rescued him. We're checking on him." *You should consider applying for adoption*, Hazel had said, right before she'd called them a nice couple. Was that how they looked to the rest of the world? Is that how the people in the busy restaurant saw them?

He hadn't been in a couple since Lillibeth, and even then he'd felt more like an accessory than a man in a relationship.

"You really are worried about him? About what will happen to him?"

He couldn't help himself. He reached out and took her hand in his again. "I would be a monster if I wasn't, Liberty."

More to the point, he'd be like his parents. They didn't worry about Marcus. They worried about whether they were maximizing the value they could get from him.

A flicker of doubt flashed over her face, but at least this

time she didn't pull her hand away. It stayed there, under his—light and warm. "We should wait a week," she finally said and he didn't miss that *we*. "Otherwise Hazel might start to get ideas. How about next Thursday? That's before you leave for the wedding."

"I suppose I don't have to ask about my schedule."

"You're fine," she said, a half grin curving her lips. Then, her gaze flicked over his body so fast that if he hadn't been watching, he would have missed it. "But the wedding is coming up fast…"

He bristled. "We're not talking about the wedding, Liberty. Not unless something changes."

"Like you deciding not to go?"

"Like you deciding to go with me."

She looked down to where they were holding hands. "I don't think that would be a very good idea," she murmured softly as she pulled her hand away.

He wanted to take her hand back, to hold on to it. He didn't. Instead he said, "I'm not even asking you as my date, you know."

She raised an eyebrow at him. "Oh, of course not. It's a legitimate business expense, no doubt."

"Having you with me when I meet with the producers the next day would be," he defended. "At the very least, you should be there for that. I'll need you to take notes."

That got her. She screwed her mouth off to one side and glowered at him. There was no other word for it. "Fine. But the wedding… Your mother would have my head on a platter, and God only knows what she'd do to you."

He sighed because he knew that was the truth. His parents might very well disown him if he went against the plan in such a public way.

But would that be so bad? For one thing, his parents' ire would be strictly private. They wouldn't dare risk the scandal of publicly disowning him. And if he was disowned, then they might very well keep their noses out of his business—for a while, at least.

"It'd be worth it to me," he told her. "Not to see your head on a platter but just to piss them off."

"I don't want to be the rope in your tug-of-war, Marcus."

"If you came with me, I would do everything in my power to make sure you weren't."

She took in a deep breath. "Why do you want me to go so badly? Why does it have to be me?"

"Because I trust you."

She looked stunned. "Why would you do that?" she asked in a quiet voice.

"Because you've earned it. Look," he said in frustration. "Trust is the one thing in this world that I literally cannot buy. I can't put a price on it. No one can. You can buy loyalty, but the risk with that is that someone else can offer a higher price for the same loyalty."

"Is this just because I didn't take Jenner's job?"

"No." This was going nowhere fast. Why couldn't he make her understand? "It's because you work weekends without letting me know. It's because you run with me every day. It's because you are the only person to tell me to do what I want instead of what you think I should do. It's because you..."

Because you care about me.

Because I care about you.

But he didn't say it. He couldn't, not with the way she was looking at him. "I don't think you should go to the wedding," she said softly. "But then, I don't think you want to go. So it's the same thing."

"It's not." He needed to run—to move. To do something other than to sit here and make an ass of himself trying to explain it to her. "And you? What do you want? You can't want to work every weekend."

She shrugged and dropped her gaze. He could feel her retreating, as if what she wanted wasn't important. But it was.

"Let me ask you this—if this wasn't Lillibeth's wedding, would you go with me?"

She didn't hesitate. "No. I don't fit in your world, Marcus. It's foolish to assume I could."

"But would you want to?"

Her mouth opened and then closed, and he knew the answer was *yes*.

"That's beside the point," she finally said but it was too late.

"What is the point?"

"We work together. We come from two different worlds. This…" She looked around at the people eating taffy balloons and drinking expensive wine. "I don't belong here, Marcus. What I want is what I have—a good job working for a good boss who trusts me."

"You don't want anything else? Something more?" That couldn't be all. Hell, as rich as he was, he still wanted.

He wanted someone he could trust with his deepest secrets, his darkest moments. He wanted a woman in his bed he could trust unequivocally, without worrying about how the story might show up on the gossip sites the next day.

He wanted someone a hell of a lot like Liberty.

Color flamed at her cheeks, but she didn't even blink as she said, "No. There's nothing else I want."

Wouldn't you know, she was the one thing money couldn't buy. "Come on," he said, tossing his napkin onto the table. "I'll take you home."

Eight

Marcus barely glanced at the bill before he paid it, which was enough to remind Liberty of the huge gulf that separated them.

Hell, an ocean the size of the Pacific separated them.

So what if the idea of a three-day weekend with him was exactly what she wanted? So what if he looked at her as if she was the woman of his dreams? So the hell what if she was physically shaking from the effort it took not to lace her fingers with his when he touched her hand?

It didn't matter what she wanted. What mattered was that she was safe and happy and had managed to make something out of her life.

Something foolish like fantasizing about Marcus, how he'd shower her with affection and gifts and make her feel like a princess—that was the quickest way to lose everything she'd fought for. And she wasn't that foolish. She didn't need to be rescued by Prince Charming. She'd already rescued herself.

She needed to get away from him, away from his pleading looks and his demands that she tell him her heart's desire.

"I'll just catch a cab," she said when they emerged onto Halstead. She was having trouble shifting her mental gears from a meal that probably cost a thousand dollars—not including tip—to her one-bedroom apartment wedged into a carriage house behind a two-flat.

Good Lord. That meal had probably been more than her rent.

She clung to that fact when Marcus came up behind her and put his hand in the small of her back, propelling her toward the valet. "I'll drive you home," he insisted.

"You don't have to do that," she said, the desperation growing. Because if he drove her home—all that time in the car together? This situation was rapidly moving beyond awkward and fast approaching dangerous.

"But I want to. It would be ungentlemanly of me to not see you home."

"Why?" Why did he insist on playing with fire?

She knew the answer, of course. It was because the flames would not burn him, not as they would her. He might get a little singed around the edges, but that would be the worst of it.

Men like Marcus Warren didn't face the same set of consequences women like Liberty Reese did. That was just a simple fact of life. He could whisper sweet nothings in her ear and kiss her and then, when the morning regret came crashing down on his head, he could simply fire her.

Well, she didn't think he'd do that, not to her. But she might suddenly have another job offer from one of his friends— Jenner, even—and this time, he'd insist she take it. For her own good, no doubt.

This was why she didn't have romantic entanglements. The risk always outweighed what little reward she might glean from a brief physical coupling.

She could not expose herself, not like that. Intimacy would lead to questions and questions and more damn questions.

She didn't want anything to change. Not at work, not between her and Marcus. She wanted him to stay firmly in his office and her fantasies to stay firmly in her head.

The valet pulled up in the Aston Martin and hopped out. He tried to get Liberty's door, but Marcus waved him off. "I've got her."

Against her better judgment, she sank down into the Aston Martin's seats and tucked her feet up so Marcus could shut the door. She watched him as he walked around the front of the vehicle. What had she done to deserve this? It wasn't just that he was gorgeous, a blond god with blue eyes and a runner's body. It wasn't even that he was so rich that money was little more than air to him.

It was that he looked at her as no one else ever had. Marcus *saw* her. She'd spent her entire adult life—and most of her adolescence—trying to be invisible. Burying herself in her homework so she could get ahead, get out of the projects, get to college—get this job. The only way anyone had ever paid any attention to her was because she was a good student and now, a good assistant. By herself, Liberty was worthless. Well, maybe not worthless. Grandma Devlin had done the best she could, and she wasn't even Liberty's grandmother. She was just a kindly old neighbor who'd lost her own children to the streets and who saw a little girl who needed help.

But Grandma Devlin was the exception that proved the rule. No one else could be bothered with Liberty Reese. She had been invisible to the world—to her own mother. She was valuable only because she made herself valuable.

Maybe too valuable. Did Marcus want her, Liberty Reese? Or did he want what he thought she represented— someone trustworthy and honest, someone who knew her place?

Because he didn't know her, not the real her.

He couldn't. Not now, especially after he'd sat there and told her all the reasons he trusted her.

She would do anything to not destroy his version of Liberty Reese. Anything.

"The address?" Marcus said in a casual tone once he was behind the wheel.

She gave him her address. "It's off of Fullerton." When he looked at her, she said, "Logan Square."

"Ah," he replied, as if he'd ever been there before. She highly doubted he had.

As he drove, she began to panic. What would he say when he saw the run-down two-flat building? When he realized she didn't even live in the building, but in the carriage house out back? Would he start in on how she should ask— no, demand—more of him? And, by extension, of herself?

He simply didn't realize how much she'd already demanded—of herself, of her world. The fact that she'd made it this far was not to be taken lightly.

"This is pretty far from the Loop," Marcus observed as they negotiated Friday-night traffic on the Kennedy.

"It's not that far, really."

"But what time do you have to leave to get to my place for the morning run?" The way he asked it made it clear that this was the first time he'd ever thought of it. "You're at my door at seven every single day."

She fought the urge to squirm in her seat. Point of fact, she was at his door at 6:50 a.m. every day. Then she stashed her backpack of work clothes in a closet where the doorman had reserved a space just for her and waited for Marcus to come down. "The Blue Line is only two blocks from my apartment," she hedged. "It's a straight shot to the Loop and then I catch a bus to your place. It's not bad. At that time in the morning, there's hardly ever any traffic jams."

"Liberty," he said in a stern voice. "I asked you a question. What time do you leave your place?"

She was trapped. "I catch the six oh nine—the train runs every five minutes," she added, as if that somehow made it better.

It didn't. "So you get up—what, at five thirty? Every morning?"

"Basically."

"And you work until six or so every night?"

"Yes," she said, getting irritated. "Do I need to account for my time in between six at night and five in the morning?"

They finally edged off the Kennedy and onto Fullerton. "No, no," he said, sounding lost in thought. "That's not it. It's just…"

"It's just that the rest of us don't have lakefront condos, personal chefs, cars and drivers, and an unlimited budget?"

"I'm not clueless, you know. I realize that very few people live like I do."

"Sure you do—as an abstraction. Have you ever been here? Or to Rogers Park? Ever ventured out of the trendy, safe areas of Chicago?"

His silence answered the question for him.

"This is what I mean, Marcus. This is why I can't go with you to that wedding, why it's ridiculous to think I should even want to. You see me in a specific set of circumstances, but that's not the whole of me. This," she said, gesturing out the window, "this is a nice neighborhood. I have a nice place. I've worked hard for it. But that's not what you're going to see."

He turned onto her street and pulled up to the curb in front of her landlord's two-flat. Then to her horror, he shut the car off and turned to face her. "What am I going to see, Liberty? What am I looking at, right now?"

Me. You're looking at me. That's what she wanted to say. This was a nice place compared with the slum she'd grown up in. This was her getting above her station in life. She'd come up so far that sometimes she looked around and got scared of the heights she now occupied.

Because what he was looking at was a nobody who dared to act as if she were a somebody.

"Money isn't air," she whispered. "Every dollar I make is spoken for. Every grocery trip I make, every lunch I pack, every pair of running shoes I buy is a risk because what if that's it? What if there's no more?"

"Then why didn't you take Jenner's job offer? Why didn't you take a bigger paycheck?"

"Because money isn't the only thing I need from this job."

Damn that truth.

The space between them was already tight. This was not a big car. But there was no mistaking it—that space was shrinking. She didn't know if she was leaning toward him or he was leaning toward her. All she knew was that his gravity was pulling her in and she couldn't fight it any more than she could decide she could fly.

"What else do you need?" he asked in a serious voice. She felt his breath whisper over her skin and she shivered.

"Marcus..." But whatever else she was going to say was cut off as he cupped her cheek in his palm and lifted her face toward his.

"Do you need something else? Something more? Because I do."

In her last grasp at the safety of the way things were, she said, "This will change everything."

His nose touched the tip of hers and she felt his fingers on her skin—pulling her toward him. "What if everything has already changed and we can't go back?"

"I'm not good for you," she warned him even as her

hands moved, touching his face, feeling the slight prick of his stubble against her palm. A sign that he wasn't some perfect god of a man but someone real and warm and hers. Hers, but not for the taking. "I'm *not*."

"Then be bad for me," he murmured against her lips.

All at once, he was kissing her and God help her, Liberty was kissing him back. Her first real kiss. She so desperately wanted to catalog each moment to remember it for all time—she was kissing Marcus Warren!

But any hope of memorizing the moment disappeared under the pressure of his skin against hers. Touching Marcus, tasting him—she couldn't think, couldn't rationalize. This was really happening, she thought over and over. Heat burned through her limbs, making her fall into him.

This was weakness, temptation—things she'd always been above because survival was more important than a kiss. But she'd come to a place where she wasn't on the ragged edge anymore—thanks to him.

His lips moved over hers gently at first and she instinctively opened her mouth for him. She wanted this—him. She was horribly afraid she might *need him*.

When his tongue swept into her mouth, she jolted in her seat. The shock of the intimacy was enough to pull her out of the moment, and the weight of what she was doing hit her like a hammer to the chest. "I can't do this," she sputtered, pulling away from him. She fumbled for the seat belt but she was so disorientated that it took several tries before she clicked the right button.

"Wait—what?" He latched onto her forearm, halting her before she could get the door open. "Can't—or won't?"

She jerked her arm out of his grasp and somehow let herself out of the car. Then she was walking up the sidewalk, her head down and her steps quick. She didn't have his money and, when he touched her like that, she didn't have much air, either.

She heard his car door open behind her but she didn't slow down and she didn't look back.

"Liberty?"

She didn't answer. What could she say? *I want you? I've fantasized about you for years? I would do anything you ask of me—just don't ask me about my past?*

He trusted her. He thought she was honest with him.

If anyone saw them together and did a little digging, she could ruin him.

And she cared too much about him to see him hurt like that.

So she walked away from him.

It was all she could do.

Nine

"Mr. Warren," the security guard said, standing to attention when Marcus walked into the building.

"Hello…" He leaned forward to read the guard's name tag. "Lester."

He knew the guards who were in the lobby every weekday, but he couldn't remember the last time he'd dropped by the office on a weekend. When he worked on the weekend, it was reading reports Liberty had prepared for him from the comfort of his sofa, usually with a game on in the background. "Were you the one I talked to earlier today?"

"Yes, sir," the older man said, still standing smartly at attention. Maybe he was a former military man?

"Ah, good. Is Ms. Reese still here?"

"Yes, sir," Lester repeated. "Ms. Liberty got here at eight thirty, like she does every Saturday."

Marcus got the feeling that Liberty wouldn't have had to look at Lester's name tag. "And she stays until…"

"Three, three thirty," Lester said warmly. "A hard worker, that one."

"Yes," Marcus agreed. He was beginning to realize exactly how hard Liberty worked.

Every Saturday for close to three years, she had worked an extra seven hours.

He definitely didn't pay her enough.

"Thanks, Lester," Marcus said, heading for the elevators.

The ride up to his floor had never felt so long. Hell, the whole morning had been long. He'd wanted to get here first thing, but even he saw the folly of that. If he burst into the office right after Liberty got there, she'd most likely panic and bolt on him.

Just as she'd done last night.

Jesus, this was a mess. And the hell of it was, he wasn't sure he'd do anything different. Well, maybe he wouldn't take her to that restaurant. But everything else?

He'd wanted to go with her to see the baby.

He'd wanted to take her to dinner.

He'd wanted to kiss her.

And what a kiss it'd been. Raw need had coursed through his body at the touch of her lips against his, her skin in his hands. He'd wanted to strip her out of her sensible skirt suit and lay her out on a bed and lavish her with attention until she was crying out his name.

He still wanted that. But he didn't think he was going to get it.

The elevator doors opened and he strode out into Warren Capital's offices. Somehow everything felt different on the weekend. The heat of summer seemed to seep in through the windows and pop music played in the background. He saw an open snack container on a desk.

Liberty was not at her desk.

Marcus stared at the empty chair, not grasping what he saw. She was here. Lester had said so. He peeked into his office—maybe she was in there? No. The place was empty. Where could she have gone?

Then behind him he heard the door to the bathroom open. Before he could turn around, Liberty exclaimed, "Marcus! What are you doing here?"

"I came to see you," he said. And then he *saw* her.

Instead of the woman in the running shorts and a shapeless unisex T-shirt or the woman in the business suits, Liberty stood before him in a short khaki skirt, flip-flops and a sleeveless shirt covered in a brightly colored pattern. The only part of her that was the same as ever was her hair, but even that was different. Instead of her polished buns or sleek ponytails, her hair was messily knotted at the nape of her neck.

She looked young and sweet and everything about her made him want to pull her into his arms and kiss her all over again.

"I didn't expect—I mean, you never come in—oh," she finally said and stopped talking. Her gaze swept up and down his body and he could guess that she was having the same reaction he was. She'd probably never seen him in a T-shirt, cargo shorts and deck shoes. She crossed her arms over her chest and rubbed her bare skin as if she were suddenly cold.

"I needed to come in today," he said, clenching his hands at his sides so he wouldn't rub her arms for her. "I needed to talk to you."

"Is this about work? I'm getting caught up."

"You work every Saturday," he reminded her, wondering why she phrased it like that. "This isn't about work. We have a problem."

"Oh?" she asked drily, which made him grin. "Only one?"

"One big problem, which spawns several smaller issues." She looked at him wryly. "And that is?"

"You care for me." She opened her mouth to say something, but he didn't give her the chance to deny it. "And I care for you."

"Oh." The word rushed out of her in a burst of air, but that was all she said. She didn't try to talk her way out of it or make excuses.

He couldn't tell if that was a good *oh* or a bad one. "Yes. And you seem to think that it's a problem."

This time, when she exhaled, it was clearly in frustration. "Because it is, Marcus. You saw where I live. You saw how I couldn't even navigate dinner at a restaurant where they know you by name. The only way our worlds ever cross is in this office or on the jogging path. It doesn't matter how I feel about you, and believe it or not, it doesn't matter how you feel about me. It simply won't work."

That answer made him mad. It didn't matter how he felt? How she felt? That sounded like something his mother would say—something she had said when the Lillibeth situation had blown up. It hadn't mattered that he'd been hurting. What had mattered was putting on a good face for the public.

"The kiss last night—are you telling me it didn't matter?"

She touched the tips of her fingers to her lips. "It doesn't change anything."

"The hell it doesn't, Liberty. Did you want to kiss me last night?" Because the thought niggled at him: Had he kissed her against her will?

He wasn't going to prey on his assistant, not as his father preyed on his secretaries.

"That's not important," she said in a shaky voice. "What I want isn't important."

"Don't give me that crap. What you want is just as important as what I want." She opened her mouth to argue with him but he wasn't having it. "Answer the damned question, Liberty. Did you want the kiss?" She looked at him as if he were making for her fingernails with a pair of pliers, but he couldn't walk away from this—from her. He had to know. "Do you want me?"

The silence hung in the air for a beat too long as they stared at each other. "Of course," she whispered, all the blood draining out of her face. "Of *course* I do. But—"

There were no *but*s here. He closed the distance between them in two long strides, pulled her into his arms and kissed her with everything he had. After a squeak of surprise, he was thrilled when Liberty sighed into his mouth, her body molding itself to his.

When the kiss ended, he looked her in the eye and brushed an errant strand of hair away from her face. "Don't tell me *that* doesn't matter, Liberty. It does. Because *you* matter to me."

She closed her eyes and breathed deeply. "It won't end well. I'm not good for you."

She'd said that last night and it'd bothered him then. It bothered him even more now. "But what if I can be good for you? No one cares about me like you do, Liberty. No one worries about what's good for me or what's bad for me. I could disappear off the face of the earth tomorrow and you know what people would mourn? They'd mourn the senseless loss of my money, my looks, my power. My parents wouldn't miss me. They'd only miss being able to use me for their own purposes. You are the one person in this world who would miss me."

It hurt to admit that out loud but not as much as it hurt to know it was 100 percent the truth.

Her eyes widened. "You don't mean that. People love you."

"Do they? Or do they just love what they think I can do for them?" He paced away from her, desperate to move, to think. "You don't know what it was like growing up in my house. Do you have any idea how crushing it is to realize that your parents don't love you? That they wouldn't fight for you, not even if you really needed them to?"

He'd learned that so early. He'd been what, six? Six years old when the men with the guns had tried to take him and his nanny. Miss Judy had screamed and chased the bad guys off and saved him. And what had his parents done? Nothing—except to get rid of his nanny.

Even now, the crushing loneliness of that time filled him with despair. He began to pace.

"I do," she said in a gentle voice, crossing to him. But she didn't try to slow him down. "More than you can know." He paused and looked at her. "But—"

"Don't you dare say it doesn't matter, Liberty. You want to know what doesn't matter? All of this. This office, this company, this life. You're so worried about my reputation and I couldn't give a rat's ass about it." He pulled up short and stared at her. He didn't know where the words were coming from. All he knew was that they'd been building up since last night—since before that, if he were honest. Ever since he'd found that little baby boy—and seen Liberty care for him.

Ever since he'd found someone he wanted to fight for.

And now that the words were coming out, there was no stopping them. "It's not me. It's not who I am. It's what they wanted me to be."

"Who did you want to be?" she asked softly.

He laughed bitterly. "Do you realize you're the first person to ask?"

"You talk like it's too late, like you don't have the power to do what you want. But that's not true, Marcus. It's never too late."

"I thought you didn't want anything to change."

She gave him a long look then, full of heartache and sorrow. "Do you think I'd be happy knowing that I was one of the wardens who kept you locked in a cage of someone else's making? Do you really think that I'd sacrifice you just so I wouldn't have to do something risky?"

"Everyone else would. Lillibeth would have."

"I'm not everyone else and I am *not* Lillibeth." This time, she was the one who crossed to him, grabbed his face in her hands and hauled him down to her lips.

It wasn't an expert kind of kiss, but that didn't matter to him. He wrapped his arms around her and clung to her as she kissed him again and again. His blood sang through his body. Nothing separated them except a few thin layers of clothes. When she nipped at his lower lip, he went hard for her.

He slammed on the brakes before they went too far. "Liberty," he groaned, holding her tight, her chest heaving against his. He felt as if he'd run a marathon in record time.

"I know who you are," she whispered against the sensitive skin of his neck.

"Do you?" Was that even possible when he wasn't entirely sure he knew?

"You're a good man, Marcus Warren." Right now, with her in his arms—her body pressed against his—he did not feel like a good man. "You treat your employees well," she went on, kissing her way up his neck. "You care about a baby that no one else does."

Her teeth skimmed over his skin right below his ear and he couldn't have fought back the groan if he'd tried. His hand slid down her back and he cupped her bottom, pushing her against him so she could feel exactly what she did to him.

He couldn't remember being this turned on.

Oh, sure, he was no innocent. He liked sex. He had his pick of beautiful women, models and actresses and heiresses, all making eyes at him from the time he'd hit puberty. Sex was easy, fun.

Or it had been, once. When had he last been this excited? When was the last time he'd wanted not just sex, but the woman?

Because this was Liberty. This wasn't just sex. This was something else entirely.

"You make me feel important," she murmured in his ear and he was powerless to stop her as she wrapped her lips around his lobe and sucked.

"You are important," he got out through gritted teeth. But when she shifted, rubbing against his erection as her hands began to drift down his backside, he forced himself to breathe again. "Is this what you want? Because if you keep kissing me like that…"

She angled his face so she could look him in the eye. "What I want," she said in all seriousness, "is to get out of this office."

Out of this office, out of these clothes—yeah, he was on board with that. "My place? Would you come home with me?"

"It'll change everything," she said, but this time she wasn't trying to warn him off. Instead, for the first time, she sounded as if she accepted that it *had* to change, that staying the same would mean a slow death for both of them.

He held her tight and buried his nose in her hair. "I want it to. I need it to."

"Then let's get out of here."

Liberty had been to Marcus's condo building, of course. Every weekday morning she waited for him in the lobby. But she'd never crossed the inlaid tile line in the lobby that divided the doorman's territory from the rest of the building, and she'd certainly never been up to Marcus's floor.

Thankfully, Joey, the usual doorman she dealt with, wasn't working at noon on a Saturday. "Todd," Marcus said to the man in the fancy coat.

"Mr. Warren," Todd replied, giving Liberty a little smile.

Jesus, she was doing this, she really was. She was crossing that little line in the tile and getting into an elevator with Marcus.

"Okay?" he asked as the doors slid shut, blocking them off from the bright lobby. He slid his arm around her waist and pulled her in close. "Still okay?"

Yes. And no, but yes. In her dreams, Marcus swept into the office and kissed her and told her how much he needed her and yes, they wound up in bed.

But now? At this exact moment?

This was stupid. This wasn't just a risk—this was practically career suicide. Yes, she wanted Marcus and yes, he wanted her and thank God they were both unattached, consenting adults.

It didn't change the fact that she was initiating a physical relationship with her boss. It didn't change the fact that she'd kissed him back.

But he was right. There was no going back to the way things were. She cared for him and he cared for her and that was a hell of a thing.

"Better than okay," she said, pulling him down for a kiss.

Marcus's lips moved over hers with an urgent pressure as he spun and backed her against the wall of the elevator. "I want you so much," he whispered in her ear as his hands slipped down her bottom. "I want to do everything you like."

Well. There was that. She didn't, technically, know what she liked. Her childhood and adolescence had been about self-preservation and besides, when a girl spent every weekend in the library, who had time for dating?

So she did what she always did—she hedged the truth. Just a little. "I want to see what you've got," she murmured. Then she boldly slipped her hand down between their bodies and over the bulge in his shorts. "Oh, my." Was that all *him*?

"Liberty," he hissed, his hips flexing against her palm. That really was all him, hot and hard and barely contained by his shorts.

The elevator came to a stop. She tensed—what if someone were waiting to get on and saw them?

But Marcus grinned down at her. "Relax, babe. I own this entire floor." He gave her another quick kiss and then pushed away, leading her out into a small room with a door. "I didn't like that the elevator opened up directly into my place," he explained as he unlocked the door. "Too much of a chance that my parents could bribe their way into the building."

He threw the bolt and exhaled in what looked like relief before he pulled her back into his arms.

"We're safe here," he told her.

Then he was kissing her again and for the first time, she let herself get fully lost in his touch. It wasn't the same fall-off-the-edge-of-the-earth sensation that she'd had in his car last night.

"Let me give you the tour," Marcus said, backing her up. She kicked off her dollar-store flip-flops and let him guide her. "This is the entryway." As he spoke, he grabbed at the hem of her shirt and started to pull.

"It's lovely," she replied, not looking at the entryway one bit. Instead, she was studying him. This—this was how they really were. Teasing and talking, just as they did on their morning runs. Except now, they were touching.

"Oh, Liberty," he said in awe as he dropped her shirt on the floor. His hands touched the sides of her waist for a brief second before he started stroking upward, over her ribs. Then he was cupping her breasts, his thumbs brushing over her plain white bra. "Look at you, babe."

Liberty shivered—actually shivered—at his touch. She wasn't clueless, just inexperienced. She'd seen men touch women and women touch men, but she hadn't quite grasped how overwhelming those touches could be.

"Good?" Marcus asked, leaning down to press a kiss to the top of her left breast, right above the bra cup.

"Keep moving," she ordered. She didn't want her first time to be in a hallway.

An image assembled itself for her, of Marcus backing her against the wall right there, lifting her up and wrapping her legs around his waist while he thrust into her.

Okay, right. Not her first time. But maybe her second time. And her third time.

"Hmm," Marcus hummed, his tone light. But he kept pushing her backward, one hand snaking down to her lower back and slipping beneath the waistband of her skirt to brush at the skin hidden there. "And here we have the sitting room. Sometimes, I sit there."

She burst out laughing. "We should maybe try it sometimes. The sitting."

"Want to try other things first," he murmured as her bra strap gave under his expert fingers. The straps slid down her arms and he tossed the bra aside. "These, for example."

He leaned down and took her right nipple in his mouth. Then he sucked.

The sensation was almost too much for her. Looking down and seeing Marcus Warren doing that to her?

But, no, she reminded herself. He was just Marcus.

She threaded her fingers through his golden hair and held him to her. Her head fell back and a low moan pulled itself from her throat. "Oh. The sitting room," she managed to say. "Got it."

"I love this room," he agreed, switching to the other breast.

"It's a great room. Great views." But her eyes had fluttered shut so she could focus on the feeling of Marcus's tongue sliding over her bare skin, of his fingers gripping into her flesh.

A flash of panic popped up out of nowhere as Marcus turned her to the left and continued to back her up. Was this really happening? Or was this a dream? The most realistic, most erotic dream she'd ever had? Maybe she'd fallen asleep at work. She hadn't slept well last night, not after bolting out of Marcus's car. She could be hallucinating this entire thing.

"Dining room," he murmured.

Liberty was only vaguely aware that they were moving through a room that contained tables and chairs. Instead, she was more focused on how Marcus's hands snaked down her hips and how he was pulling her skirt up. "Wait," she said and the moment the word left her mouth, he froze.

"Wait?" In that moment when he stopped, she fell a whole lot more in love with him. It wasn't an act. He wasn't telling her how special, how important she was just to get her in bed. He really did want her and he really did want to do right by her.

"Don't pull it up," she told him. She didn't want a boring khaki skirt bunched up around her middle. Nothing sexy about that. In her fantasies, he stripped her bare. "Just take it off."

"Woman," he growled, relief flooding his face. Whereas he'd been slow and gentle with her shirt and her bra, he jerked at the button at the top of her skirt with an almost savage force.

He didn't even get the zipper the whole way down before he was pushing at the skirt, sliding it over her hips. The fabric hit the ground with a dull *whump* and Liberty took a mental second to thank the laundry gods that she'd put on a cute pair of undies today, white with little pink flowers printed on them and an edge of lace all the way around.

"Office," he said, jerking his head at a doorway.

"Mmm," she hummed, pulling him up and working at the buttons on his shirt. Which was not easy, as she was walking backward and he was sliding his fingertips under the leg bands of her panties and kissing her neck. She managed to get the top two undone before she gave up and jerked the shirt over his head.

"Look at *you*," she whispered, running her hands over Marcus's bare chest. "Do you have any idea how long I've dreamed about this?" She rubbed her thumbs over his flat nipples.

He shuddered into her touch. "I didn't want to be that boss," he said, pivoting her to the left this time. "I didn't want to hurt you."

This was going to hurt, in the end. Not the sex so much— although it might—but falling into bed with Marcus would, in the long run, be bad for both of them.

But not falling into bed with him right now? That wasn't even an option. "Then don't hurt me," she told him, trying to unbutton his shorts.

"Bedroom," he grunted, picking her up. "Bed." The next thing she knew, Marcus was laying her out on a massive bed with crisp white sheets.

Liberty fell back, surrendering herself to the plush softness of his bed and the hard muscles of his body. She touched him everywhere, but it wasn't enough—he still had his shorts on. "I like your bedroom. Nice place."

"Better with you in it." Liberty got the button on his shorts undone but when she went for his zipper, her hands brushing his massive bulge, he sucked in a breath and grabbed her hands. "Slow down, babe. Let me just…"

He pinned her hands to the bed and kneed between her legs. "Let me learn you," he murmured, leaning down and sucking on her nipple.

"Oh, Marcus," she moaned as he kissed and sucked at her. In all the times she'd thought about this, she'd never taken into consideration the wet warmth of his mouth. All that light and heat that flowed around her focused on where his mouth touched her, and her nipple went hard under his attention.

"You like that, don't you?"

"Yes," she hissed as his mouth closed over her other nipple, pulling and tugging until she was writhing on the mattress. *"Yes."*

"You taste so good," he said as his mouth moved lower. He let go of her hands and slid his palms down her sides, hooking into the waistband of her panties. "I want to taste all of you."

He pulled and her panties came off. She was nude before him. She'd have thought that she might feel nervous or self-conscious about this—being naked, having Marcus look at her with that lust in his eyes. But she wasn't.

A strange pressure was building up inside her, like lightning getting ready to strike. She shimmied against the bed when Marcus put his hand over her heart and let his fingertips drift over her midsection. "I'm going to touch you here," he said as his hand moved lower.

"You better," she replied, impressed at how confident she managed to make that sound. He was in no hurry, though, and the anticipation was killing her. She fisted her hands in the sheets.

"Impatient? That's not like you, Ms. Reese," he said with a confident grin.

"I just want to do—" She gasped as his fingers stroked over her sex. "I just want to do a good job, Mr. Warren," she managed to say through clenched teeth as he started to rub her.

"Oh, I have no doubts that you'll do an excellent job, Ms. Reese. You always take care of everything I need, don't you?" His other hand came up between her legs and touched her opening, but he didn't stop rubbing.

"I want to be good for you," she whispered, unable to look away from where he was touching her.

"You are," he said, his voice ragged with need. "So let me be good for you."

One of his fingers slid into her.

"Oh." She sucked in air as he moved inside her and rubbed outside her. "Oh, Marcus."

"That's it, babe," he said, his own breathing coming in hard, fast bursts. "Open up for me."

Then he leaned down and his mouth replaced the finger rubbing against her and he was licking her and stroking into her, and everything about her tightened down until a wave of electricity spiked through her and her mouth fell open in a silent scream of pleasure.

It was unlike anything she'd ever felt. She'd touched herself, but those little pops of release had nothing on the way Marcus had effortlessly brought her to orgasm.

Marcus knew it, too. He looked up from between her legs and stared at her. She was powerless to do anything but stare back as her muscles pulsed around his fingers. "Ms. Reese," he said, but that was as far as he got because Liberty had grabbed hold of his face and hauled him up to her mouth.

This was what she'd guarded herself from for so long—this feeling of his weight pressing her back against the mattress, the feel of his mouth on hers, the sound of her name on his lips.

She was his now. She'd always been his.

But now?

Now he knew it, too.

Ten

The taste of Liberty still on his tongue, Marcus forced himself to push back. *Mine*, he wanted to say as he looked over her body, splayed before him with delicious wantonness. *Mine*.

Condoms. He needed condoms before he lost what little control he had. He managed to get them out of the bedside table as she was pushing his shorts off him, pulling his briefs down and going, "Oh, *Marcus*," when he sprang free.

"Babe," he managed to say, but then she wrapped her hands around him and stroked up, then down, and he lost all thought except the sensation of Liberty's hands on his shaft. He couldn't *not* move. He thrust into her hands and braced himself against the side of the bed and thrust harder.

"Do you like this?" she asked, and he didn't miss the almost innocent note to that question.

"God, yes," he groaned. It would have been easy to just go on and lose it right there in her hands, but he wasn't going to be selfish about this.

He managed to pry her hands away from his throbbing erection and roll the condom on. She watched the whole process with wide eyes. "What position works for you?" he asked, finally climbing into the bed. Before she could even answer, he pulled her into his arms and kissed the hell out of her.

Her hands were all over his body, her fingers digging into his backside—urging him on. She rolled onto her back and pulled him with her. "Like this," she said.

"Anything you want, babe." Her lower lip tucked up under her teeth as he positioned himself at her entrance, and for a second she looked so nervous that he paused. "Okay? Yes?"

"Yes," she said decisively, flexing her hips to rise up and meet him.

Marcus tried to go slowly, tried to hold himself back as he joined his body to hers. It should have been easy—for years, he'd always been able to restrain himself when it came to sex. He'd convinced himself it was because he was a considerate lover, always putting his partner's needs first.

But the truth of the matter was, it'd been safer that way, safer to make sure he didn't get hurt. Even with Lillibeth, the woman he'd resigned himself to marry, he'd never given himself over to uncontrolled passion like this. Maybe because there hadn't been all that much passion in the first place.

He trusted Liberty with his life. And he couldn't hold himself apart from her. Not any longer.

She sucked in a hot breath when he sank home into her tight body, so he kissed her and let the feeling of her warmth surround him.

Then he began to move. Liberty made little gasping noises as she clung to him, her hands digging into his shoulders, her lips on his neck, his mouth. Every so often she would move in a different way and he'd have to pause and realign, but after a while, they learned each other's pacing better and she began to rise up to meet his thrusts.

And he was lost in her. The only thing that kept him from going over the edge was his runner's stamina. He pushed himself past the point of pleasure and pain as his muscles burned and his lungs cried out for more air.

She made a noise high in the back of her throat and then her shoulders came off the bed. She clung to him before she fell back, panting and moaning his name. He couldn't hold back any longer, not when she looked up at him, her eyes glazed with desire and satisfaction.

He groaned through his climax and collapsed, his heart racing. "Liberty," he whispered into her hair. He had things he wanted to say, things he needed to tell her. But he didn't have the words—that's how lost he was.

She leaned back, her gaze searching his face. Then, when he continued to fail to come up with a single sweet nothing to whisper, she kissed him hard.

For the first time in a long time, he felt right. Definitely since Lillibeth's betrayal but even before then. He was safe here.

Liberty lay on her back, staring up at the ceiling. "So… wow."

"Yeah, wow." He grinned. "Just think—we'll have three days to do that when we go to the wedding."

The moment the words left his mouth, he realized that hadn't been the right thing to say. He felt her body tense up, felt her withdraw from him. She cleared her throat. "Um, I need to get cleaned up, I think."

"Through that door," he said, pointing to the master bath. She scooted off the bed without looking at him.

He stared at her retreating form until the bathroom door shut with a decisive click. Bringing her to his place and making love to her *had* changed everything. There was something between them, something that ran deeper and truer than anything he'd ever felt before.

It wasn't a feeling that he wanted on a part-time basis. He couldn't go back to running with Ms. Reese in the morning and working with her in the afternoon and pretend that what they'd had here didn't exist during business hours.

If they were going to be together, they were going to be *together*. Marcus Warren didn't settle.

He hurried to the bathroom down the hall, took care of the condom and cleaned up quickly, and then headed back to the bedroom. He didn't have anywhere he needed to be and there was no way in hell that he was going to let Liberty head back to the office, no matter how much she thought she needed to get ahead.

He was pulling the covers down when the bathroom door opened. Liberty, in all her nude glory, leaned against the door frame, one arm seductively wrapped around her waist. Marcus was glad to see the satisfied little smile on her face, glad to know he'd given that to her.

"Hi," she said in a quiet voice.

He patted the bed next to him. "Come here."

He watched her as she crossed to him. Her body was beautiful in a real way that he wasn't sure he'd ever appreciated before. Lillibeth had had her nose fixed and her boobs enlarged and she worked out slavishly to keep her weight a ridiculous 115 pounds. Lying in bed with her had sometimes been like lying in bed with a bag of bones, all pointy and hard.

Liberty had curves. Her hips were a sight to behold and, as she slid into bed next to him, he was already having a hard time keeping his hands off them. Her nipples were far darker than he'd been expecting, but he liked them, and her breasts, although small, were more than enough to fill his hand.

He pulled her against him and touched her breast. "I can feel your heartbeat," he murmured as he pulled the covers up over them.

She put her hand on his chest. Amazing how even that simple touch warmed him. "Yours, too." She leaned forward and kissed his chest. "So, what happens next?"

"A couple of options. We could stay in bed for the next several days."

She leaned back to give him a sharp look. "You know that's not going to work."

"You're not going back to the office today and that's final," he told her. "I'll fire you if you do."

"Again with the threats," she murmured, but she didn't sound menaced. If anything, she sounded sleepy. Warm and content. And although Marcus didn't nap, per se, he felt his eyelids drifting shut as they snuggled deeper into the covers. "Fine. Twist my arm. I guess I'll just have to stay here with you."

"That's option two—the best option," he agreed, curling his body around hers. He realized he was stroking her perfect little breast, his fingers drawing over her skin toward her stiff nipple.

"What's the third option?" she asked warily.

"I understand why you're nervous about the wedding, so I can call my personal shopper and we can get some things for you. That way you won't have to worry about finding something to wear. Eventually," he added, kissing her bare shoulder.

Her hand covered his as he still stroked her breast. "Marcus... Why do you want me to go so badly?"

"Because." She didn't respond to this unhelpful comment. She just waited.

Now it was his turn to roll onto his back and stare at his ceiling. "Do you know what I wanted to be when I grew up?"

"No." She nestled into him, her hand on his chest, right over his heart. "I take it billionaire investor wasn't it?"

"No. I was actually scouted. I had scholarship offers for soccer, track and baseball from a bunch of different schools with really good programs. Not that I needed the scholarships."

"But coaches wanted you."

"They did. I had an offer from a few teams in Europe to come play soccer. Germany, I remember. There were two teams in Germany that wanted me. There was a bidding war, even."

"Really?" She leaned up on her elbow and looked down at him. "How come I don't know this? I mean, before I took the job, I googled you pretty hard."

"Nothing ever came of it. My parents didn't approve. It simply wasn't done," he said, in a reasonably good impression of his mother's simper.

Liberty winced. "Beneath a Warren?"

That made him smile. She got him in such a fundamental way. He threaded his fingers into her hair. It was coarser than he'd thought, but that just made him like it more—an extra layer of sensation. "Exactly. A few words from my father and the scholarship offers were rescinded. I have no idea how he made the Europeans go away, but he did."

"Wait—what do you mean, he made them go away?"

"I was going to go. I was eighteen and all the college offers disappeared and I had had it. I was going to go to Germany, as far away from my parents as possible, and play soccer for a few years. College could wait, right?"

She was staring at him now, the concern on her face obvious. "So, what—you decided to play professional soccer and because your father didn't approve, he made the team rescind the offer?"

"Basically. I never did know for sure, but I suspect he actually bought the team I chose—for a short while anyway."

"How could they do that to you?" She was genuinely shocked.

He smiled bitterly. "For my own good, they said. To protect me."

"What on earth would they need to protect you from so badly they had to buy a soccer team in Germany?"

"Well…" He opened his mouth to tell her about the men and the guns and losing his nanny, Miss Judy. But the words didn't come. So he didn't answer the question. Instead, he said, "It wasn't to protect me. It was to protect the family name. I went to Columbia instead and Northwestern for business school. It was literally the only option they left open for me. Everything else has been their idea."

She thought about this for a while. "Is that why you hired me? Because it wasn't your parents' idea?"

"Well, that and you said in your interview that you jogged two miles every day."

The corner of her mouth quirked up a bit. "I did, didn't I? I'm a lot faster now."

He grinned at her as he ran his hands up and down her back. "I like running with you. It's the best time of my day. You and me and the jogging path along the lake."

Her smile was wistful, almost. "It's my favorite part of the day, too."

He leaned up to kiss her because that honest touch of his lips to hers said what he couldn't seem to find the words to say.

"I want you to come with me, babe," he told her when the kiss ended. He brushed her hair back from her face and cupped her cheek. "When I'm with you, it's like I can still see that man I thought I'd be once, and I don't want to fall into line and do what I'm told, only do what's good for the family image. I want to fight for you."

She leaned into his touch. "I won't fit in your world," she warned him. "I'm not good for you." But again, it didn't sound as if she was arguing with him. It sounded as though she was accepting this fact just as she accepted that the sky was blue.

"You keep saying that." He leaned up on his elbows to stare at her. "So you're not a trust-fund baby. You keep your private life private and you've got my respect."

She didn't reply, except to look at him with her big, dark eyes.

A whisper of doubt crept into the edge of his mind. She did keep her private life private—so private, in fact, that after three years, he'd seen where she lived only last night.

In his mind, Liberty was this beacon of honesty and respectability, always on time and under budget, outperforming herself every quarter. But what if…

What if there were something she kept hidden, something that could hurt him?

He looked at her. She was lying on his stomach, her chin resting on her hands as she looked right back at him. "Do you really want to know?"

"Only if you want to tell me. The past is in the past, babe. As long as you didn't kidnap or murder anyone…" He paused.

She laughed out loud. "Good Lord, no. I have led a remarkably crime-free life. Never even been arrested."

He exhaled a breath he hadn't realized he'd been holding. She was safe and he trusted her. She was just going to have to get used to it. "You may not be good for Marcus Warren, billionaire," he conceded. "But," he went on, "you are very good for me. Come with me. Let me fight for you."

She broke eye contact first, tilting her head to the side

and resting it on his chest. "No one has ever fought for me," she said in a voice so quiet he had to lean up to catch all the words.

"No one? What about your parents?"

She shrugged. It was a seemingly casual gesture, but he could see the tension in her shoulders. He stroked her bare skin.

"As you said, it's in the past. I don't like to talk about it. But if you want me to tell you, I will."

"You don't have to. It won't change how I feel about you. I want you to be happy."

She traced a small circle on his chest with the tip of her finger. "Is that the reason you're looking out for William? Because of me?"

"Yes. But it's not the only reason. It's…" He sighed. "It's because you care about him, but it's also because when I see you with him—I didn't anticipate how it would make me feel."

She propped herself up and stared at him. "Yeah?"

What if… That's what he'd thought looking at her with that tiny baby, the love on her face obvious. "Watching you hold him, feed him—it's like I was looking at this other life, the path I didn't get to take. Maybe in another life…"

In another life, he might have already married for love, not for power or reputation. He might have a baby, or a bunch of kids, and they'd do normal things such as spend every Saturday running around soccer fields and cooking dinners together, and then he'd help put the kids to bed and pull Liberty into bed and…

"But he's African American," Liberty said, her tone careful. "Does that bother you?"

Marcus shook away the image of him and Liberty and one big, happy family. "It might bother my parents. I couldn't care less."

She continued looking at him, her eyes full of what he hoped like hell was love. Normally, when women made eyes at him, it was because of his money, his looks—or some combination of the two.

But the way Liberty looked at him was different. God, how he wanted it to be different.

"We'll go see him before we leave, okay?" he said. It was so odd. She didn't want anything from him for herself—she was adamant about that. But she wanted someone to fight for the baby. "Thursday. But I'll have my assistant check my schedule."

That got a huge grin out of her. "I think it can be arranged."

"And you'll come with me to the wedding? As my date?" He held his breath because if she said no, he would have to let it drop.

She sighed, a world-weary noise that almost made him rescind the offer. He'd backed her into a corner and it was maybe too selfish of him to ask this of her. "It's important to you?"

"You're important to me."

The corners of her eyes crinkled and he thought she might be smiling at him. Unexpectedly, she rolled off him and sat up on the edge of the bed. He wanted to pull her back down into his arms, but instead, he leaned forward and pressed a kiss between her shoulder blades, high on her back. "Then I guess we have to go shopping. I don't have a thing to wear."

Eleven

"This," Liberty said, staring down at the orange designer bikini covered in huge flowers, "is *ridiculous*."

Cathy, the Barneys New York saleslady in charge of transforming Liberty into a member of the upper crust, met her eye in the mirror of the private dressing room. "The rehearsal dinner has a theme," she reminded her. "Beach Blanket Bingo. Everyone is supposed to dress like something from an Annette Funicello movie."

"Well?" Marcus called out from the other side of the curtain.

"Do I at least get a cover-up?" Something to hide her hips would be nice. Like pants.

Cathy selected a drapey cover-up with an orange-tinted peacock-feather pattern. Liberty slipped it over her head, careful to avoid looking at the price tag. She didn't want to know. Ignorance was bliss.

What didn't help in any of this was the way the space between her legs throbbed gently with every movement, a constant physical reminder of how much things had changed.

After years of fantasizing about Marcus, she'd finally had him—her first. She hadn't had her virginity taken by force or coercion, which had always been a threat when she'd been younger and growing up with very few people to watch over her. She'd given herself to Marcus freely, and he'd done the same.

So why did she feel so damn weird about the whole thing?

Finally dressed, Liberty pushed the curtain aside and strode out into the sitting room. Marcus was reclining on a leather love seat, drinking champagne and generally looking as if he was having fun. Of course he was. He wasn't the one being trussed up like a Christmas goose.

"Like I said, ridiculous. Is this normal? For the entire guest list to be invited to a—a what? A bonfire the night before the wedding?"

Not that she would know what a normal wedding looked like—she didn't. She'd ordered gifts delivered to other people's weddings on Marcus's behalf, but she'd never been to a wedding, normal or extravagant.

Nor had she ever been to a store like Barneys. She'd thought they might be going to one of the stores on the Magnificent Mile, and that alone had been mildly overwhelming—but at least she'd been in Bloomingdale's a few times, stalking the sale rack for those few good pieces that could carry the rest of her clearance wardrobe through.

Barneys, on the other hand, was so far out of her comfort zone that the only thing she could do to keep from hyperventilating was to focus on exactly how ridiculous this entire thing was.

"Who demands that their guests show up in bikinis?" she asked, stalking to the dais in the center of the room so she could model for Marcus.

"You're lucky Lillibeth's not getting married in Vienna like the wedding I went to a few years ago. The dress code for that was lederhosen and dirndls for the women."

Liberty dropped her head into her hands. "I don't even want to know what a dirndl is, do I?"

"Probably not," he agreed. Then he added, "I'd like to see the bikini, please."

She scowled at him in the mirror. "I don't have a bikini body. I won't take the cover-up off at this party."

"You have a body. You're wearing a bikini. Ergo, you have a bikini body," he said. "Besides, if you don't go swimming in the ocean with me, you'll have to stay on the beach making small talk with all the other women who claim they don't have bikini bodies, hmm? I believe there will be surfboards and paddle boards available, as well."

"You don't fight fair." Liberty scowled harder, but she pulled the cover-up over her head. "And what will you be wearing?"

"Board shorts and a Hawaiian shirt. I won't swim in the shirt," he added. To Cathy, he said, "What shoes would you pair with that?"

Cathy disappeared back into the changing room, where racks and racks of clothing had been waiting for their arrival after Marcus had called ahead.

Liberty fought the urge to chew on her thumbnail. She was wearing a swimsuit that probably cost as much as two weeks' rent. Maybe three. "Aren't there sharks in the ocean? Things that sting and bite?"

Marcus snorted, his gaze traveling over her nearly naked body. Liberty didn't know whether to cover up or pose. "Of course. But trust me, the ocean will be much safer than the land."

Cathy reappeared with a pair of gladiator-style sandals in one hand, flip-flops in the other. Liberty dutifully put a foot in each style of shoe and stood while Marcus decided on the flip-flops. And of course the look had to be paired with huge gold earrings and a collar-style necklace and some gold bangles, according to Cathy.

Liberty winced as she was draped in finery. And she kept right on wincing as she spent the next hour and a half trying on dresses suitable for a beach wedding. If all the clothing had been pretty, that might have been one thing. But some of it wasn't pretty. Some of it—like a maxi dress that looked as though it'd been sewn out of old curtain sheers, as if she'd attempted high fashion on her own—was just hideous.

Finally, Cathy picked up a bright coral dress that was sleeveless with an asymmetrical hem. The neck was a high twist halter that tied in the back in a huge, drapey bow.

The dress was *pretty*. More important, Liberty didn't feel like an imposter in it.

Marcus knew it, too. When she walked out into the sitting room, he sat up and whistled. "Wow," he said in what sounded like awe.

"That color is fabulous with her skin tone," Cathy agreed warmly. "And since she'll be walking on the beach..." She scurried back for the gladiator sandals.

Liberty examined herself in the mirror. The dress made her seem tall and elegant—willowy, even. The color was good with her skin—she was glowing.

It didn't look like her. It looked like some alternate-reality Liberty, one who'd had a normal childhood, and a loving set of parents, and hadn't had to claw and fight for every single thing.

For the first time in a very long time, Liberty realized how much she resembled her mother. Not the woman who couldn't stay clean and out of jail, but there'd been one time...

"Mama, why do you look so pretty?" That was what

Liberty had asked. She must have been around nine. Mama had gotten clean during her first stint in prison and she'd been trying.

"I've got a date with Prince Charming, baby girl, and he's going to save me from…this," Jackie had said as their neighbor from two floors down had zipped Jackie into the borrowed pencil skirt and Grandma Devlin had unrolled the hot rollers from her hair. Mama had had "good enough hair," as she'd called it. She'd claimed her mother was half-white and that was why Liberty's hair was so good. No mention was made of Liberty's father, who was probably white, as well. But that was only Liberty's guess. They didn't speak of her father. Ever.

"Real proud of you, sweetie," Grandma Devlin had said as she teased a curl into a voluminous wave.

It was the only time Liberty had ever glimpsed the woman her mother could have been, if only she'd tried to save herself instead of expecting someone else to do it for her. Her date hadn't saved her. Maybe nothing could have.

And now here stood Liberty, wearing a four-thousand-dollar dress that was made of the softest silk and feeling as if she was trying to be something she wasn't. Was this how her mother had felt that night? In three days—or, more specifically, after three days at this destination wedding—would Liberty still be swept off her feet by a prince who promised to fight for her?

Or would she be right back where she started, waiting for life to smack her down for daring to get above her station?

Marcus stood, breaking her reverie. God, she didn't want life to smack her down again. She didn't need this Prince Charming to rescue her—she could save herself. But was it wrong to want more out of life than to just survive? Was it wrong to want something more than just an afternoon or a long weekend with Marcus?

He was looking her over and she struck a pose, mimicking the way she'd seen models stand.

"Do you like it?" he asked.

She smiled at him in the mirror. He was plunking down God-only-knew how much money on a wardrobe for her. He could just decree it was fine or not. But he still asked her opinion. "I do, actually. It doesn't feel like a costume, you know?"

"Cathy, I'll need a new tie," he said when she came back into the room.

"You went with a linen suit, correct?" Cathy said, which made Liberty look at her sideways.

"Yes," Marcus said, clearly unsurprised that the saleslady would recall his clothing options.

"I think we have something that will complement her outfit beautifully," Cathy said as she hurried from the room.

The moment the door was closed, Marcus stepped up onto the dais with Liberty. "You look gorgeous," he told her, leaning forward to press a kiss against her bare shoulder. He caught her eye in the mirror and slid his arm around her waist. "You do fit in my world, you see? You fit with me."

"It's just the dress," she said, feeling a little weird because she was wearing a gown and he was still in cargo shorts. "It's a great dress."

"It's not the dress. It's you. Babe, I know this makes you nervous, but what's the worst that will happen?" She gave him a suspicious look in the mirror, which made him grin. "You'll be your normal confident, capable self, and we'll have some fun together and *maybe* a few bored, vicious people make snide comments. So what? There's nothing inherently scandalous about you."

She swallowed. There'd been a moment this afternoon,

lying in his arms, listening to him tell her his deepest secrets, that she'd wanted to tell him hers.

And he'd said the past was the past. So it wouldn't matter that Jackie Reese had been African American or an addict or a hooker in her free time. It wouldn't matter that Liberty was a foster kid. None of it would change his opinion of her, right?

Maybe she was foolish, but she desperately wanted to believe that. He hadn't asked for details, so she hadn't told him. It wasn't dishonest because she would tell him if he asked.

"I know how these things go," Marcus went on, his fingers drifting over her bare arms. "I've weathered worse, remember? It'll only be a few short days and then people will move on to the next scandal."

She could still stop this. She could come down with the plague or something—anything to make sure that her past couldn't be used against him.

But she'd backed herself into a hell of a corner and she had no choice but to brazen it out in a pretty dress. Still, she gave him one final out. "Are you sure about this?" she asked even as she leaned into him. "It's not too late. We could just spend the three days in bed here."

He turned her into his arms and looked her in the eye. "We still have time before the trip, if you want to come home with me."

"You mean, spend the night?" She'd be lying if she said the idea didn't appeal to her. A night curled around Marcus? Waking up by his side in his gorgeous home, the lake spread out beneath them?

It was like something out of a fairy tale.

He cupped her face. "Yes. It's fine if you don't but…" Then he lowered his lips and kissed her. Her blood began to pound and the space between her legs throbbed even harder. It wasn't a bad thing, that throbbing. If only he'd touch her there again, take some of the pressure off her body as he'd done earlier... "I want you to stay."

How could she refuse? "I'll need to go back to my apartment at some point before work on Monday," she said in a quiet voice. "I'll need my running shoes. I have this boss, you see..."

His eyes lit up with hope—and excitement. "We can stop by after this, then grab some dinner."

"Not at that fancy restaurant?"

"No," he quickly agreed. "Let's get some takeout and watch the sun set. Just you and me. Let me show you how good I can be for you."

"Here we are," Cathy announced loudly as the door cracked open. Liberty jumped and tried to step clear of Marcus, but he didn't let her go and Cathy didn't come rushing in. "This tie will match her dress perfectly, but I brought a few others, just in case. I've got pocket squares and sock options, as well."

Marcus barely looked at the ties before giving his approval to the first one. Then, stepping off the dais, he said, "I think that we're ready to move forward."

Twelve

This time, when Marcus and Liberty got out of the car in front of the little bungalow in Rogers Park, they held hands as they walked to the door.

It was a brilliantly hot Thursday afternoon, one of those days that's so warm the sky is no longer blue but a nearly colorless gray. It was the kind of day when Liberty stayed at work as long as she could. She was lucky she had a window air conditioner in her apartment, but air-conditioning wasn't cheap. She ran it only when she was home.

Of course, she hadn't exactly been at home much in the past six days. And she hadn't been working late in the office, either. Instead, she'd spent nearly every moment with Marcus.

The whole week had a dreamlike quality to it. Dining out at nice—but not too weird—restaurants with Marcus. Going to see a White Sox game Tuesday evening. Even the morning runs were different. She ran faster because instead of having to catch the train to work to shower, she raced Marcus back upstairs to his home and they showered—together.

But the thing about dreams was that they always ended sooner or later. And since they were flying out on Marcus's private jet early tomorrow morning for that wedding—the wedding she had a completely new wardrobe for—she was afraid that the ending would definitely be sooner.

And it would be no one's fault but her own.

The door popped open before Marcus could ring the bell. "Mr. Warren!" Hazel Jones stood in the open doorway, beaming a megawatt smile at them. "Ms. Reese! Oh, it's just…" Her voice trailed off as honest-to-goodness tears formed in her eyes.

"What's wrong? Is William okay?" Liberty demanded, releasing Marcus's hand and rushing toward the older woman.

She was surprised when Hazel pulled her into a hug. "It's just the most wonderful thing ever!" she said in a quavering voice. "William's fine, just fine. Do come in."

"I trust everything was delivered satisfactorily?" Marcus asked as Hazel began her slow climb up the flight of stairs. Liberty paused and looked back at him.

"What did you do?" she asked in a whisper as he pushed the door shut.

Marcus winked at her. "You'll see."

"I know you called," Hazel was saying, "but I had no idea you meant to replace it all. And when the men showed up! Oh, my heavens!"

"Replace *what*?" Liberty whispered at him. But his only response was to place his hand on her lower back and propel her forward.

"William's just waking up," Hazel said as she disappeared into the nursery. "Oh, those men did such a quick job—I hardly had to worry about a thing!"

"What…" Liberty walked into the nursery and her words died on her lips.

The walls were the same, with all the curled and faded photos of tiny babies tacked up. But the rest of the room?

Gone were the rickety metal swing and the metal crib. Gone was the dresser that doubled as a changing table and the second crib. The ancient rocker that had barely rocked wasn't there anymore, either.

Everything was brand-new. There were two sturdy wooden cribs finished in a high-sheen gloss. Instead of threadbare cotton sheets, there was new bedding and, Liberty was willing to bet, new mattresses. The swing was up-to-the-minute and the rocker was so clean that it practically glowed. The changing table was an actual table now, with stacks of diapers underneath. The dresser next to the table matched the cribs and the rocker.

"This is simply the most thoughtful thing anyone has ever done for me," Hazel said, clasping her hands in front of her as if she were giving thanks to God.

"It was nothing," Marcus said warmly, moving toward the crib where William was beginning to fuss. "You're doing so much good in this world, helping these babies out. I just wanted to make your life a little easier."

Then, as Liberty stared at him, he leaned over and picked William up—correctly, even, supporting his head and everything. "Hey there, buddy," he said in a soft voice. "Did you grow? I think you grew!" He tucked William into his arms and began to sway gently from side to side. "How do you like your new swing?"

Something clenched in Liberty's stomach, some need she couldn't even name. As she watched, completely dumbstruck, William blinked and focused on Marcus. His little mouth opened and he made a sighing sound. It was a noise of contentment.

A hundred images flooded her mind—images she knew she couldn't have, but she wanted anyway. A baby—not just any baby, but their baby. And Marcus would be right there with her. He wouldn't disappear and abandon them. They'd get up in the morning and load the child into the jogging stroller and they'd all run together and then, when he got older, they'd spend Saturdays at the parks, playing soccer and baseball. Afternoons on the beach, trips to the museums.

What she wanted more than anything else in the world was a family—with Marcus, with William, with babies of their own. A family where no one had to hide from drug dealers or pimps or even overbearing parents. A family where they had lots of good food and a nice place to live and they never had to worry about tomorrow. A family where everyone was happy and laughing and smiling.

She'd always wanted that, ever since she'd realized that other people had it.

But now? Watching Marcus coo at William?

She wanted that with them. The wanting was so strong that she couldn't even seem to breathe.

"Those men—they even washed the bottles!" Hazel was saying. "I never! They put everything together, took all the old things away and even organized the drawers!"

Marcus turned to her. "Was everything acceptable? Is there anything I missed? I don't really know what a baby needs, so I had to take the salesman at his word."

"My heavens!" Hazel wiped a tear of joy from her eye. "It's so much more than I could give the little angels." She turned to Liberty. "Did you help pick out the clothing? So thoughtful, to send clothing for little boys and little girls."

Liberty realized that her mouth was hanging open to her chin. She shook her head, trying to make sense of all of this.

Marcus, who had just spent maybe ten thousand dollars on a weekend wardrobe for her, had at some point spent another God-only-knew how much on a complete nursery, including bottles and clothes. And all for an abandoned baby boy he had no earthly reason to care for.

"No," Liberty finally said, her voice weak. "He did this all."

"Why," Hazel said, turning her attention mercifully back to Marcus, "you're just a guardian angel, aren't you?" William made a high whining noise in the back of his throat. "Oh," Hazel said, "he's hungry. I'll go get his bottle and you can feed him."

"Okay," Liberty said. Somehow, despite the fairy-tale qualities of the past six days, this took the cake. When Hazel was out of earshot, she turned to Marcus. "*When* did you do this? *How* did you do this?"

The man had the nerve to look pleased with himself as he sat in the chair and began to rock William. "I wanted it to be a surprise. Before I came to find you at the office last Saturday, I made some calls."

"*Why* did you do this, Marcus?"

He gave her a long look. "You have to ask?"

"Here we are," Hazel said, bustling back in. "Oh, just look at the two of you," she added, beaming down at William and Marcus. "Don't they make a handsome pair?"

"They do," Liberty agreed automatically.

The panic hit her like a Mack truck barreling down the highway at seventy miles an hour, and suddenly she couldn't breath. This was all well and good, this little delusion she and Marcus were enjoying. All of her private fantasies were not only seeing the light of day, but Marcus was proving to be better than she ever could have dreamed. She knew sex was fun—why else did people do it so much? But being in bed with Marcus, where she could pretend their world was just big enough for the two of them—that was one thing.

But this? Him sending professional baby people over to revamp Hazel's house? Him taking her for a wardrobe makeover so she could fit into his world—no, not even that. So she could fit into a very specific social setting, complete with cheating ex-girlfriend and overbearing, borderline abusive parents?

No. Not only was this not going to work, was this going to fail—it was going to fail epically. Marcus may think that a few vicious people might whisper behind their hands at this wedding and then people would move on, but Liberty knew the truth. People didn't move on from something like this.

She'd come so far. She'd literally, figuratively and metaphysically pulled herself up by her own bootstraps through the sheer force of her will and a promise she'd made to Grandma Devlin all those years ago—she would save herself. Because no one else would do it for her. Not her mother, not her nonexistent father—not even Grandma Devlin could save Liberty from her own mother or from foster care.

But Liberty had gone too far. She'd fallen in love with a billionaire—someone so far above her station that she shouldn't have even been able to see him, much less talk with him, work with him—run with him. She'd gotten too close to the sun and when the truth burned bright, she would fall back to earth and her carefully constructed life would fall with her.

For so long, that had always been the worst thing that could happen to her—someone would learn the truth and she'd be out of a job, back on the streets, struggling to start over once again. But now she knew the real truth.

Marcus looked up at her as if he could sense her racing thoughts. "Liberty?"

"I'm sorry," she said, her voice shaky. Because she was. When she fell, she wouldn't just lose her job. She'd lose Marcus. She'd hurt him because he was naive enough to think that he could trust her.

"I asked if you two had discussed applying for adoption." If a little old lady could do puppy-dog eyes, Hazel was doing them right now. "William would be lucky to have two loving parents like you." She sighed happily. "Such a handsome family you'd be."

Marcus looked at Liberty as if he were expecting her to come up with some sort of reasonable response to this statement, but she had nothing. So he finally said, "We're still thinking about it."

Oh, God—he *was* thinking about it. She could tell from the way he gazed down on William's little face as he happily drank his milk.

And just as she'd stood in front of that mirror and seen a different version of her mother—a path not taken—she knew that right now, Marcus was looking at a different version of himself, one where he found a way to make her fit into his life and a way to make this baby fit into his life and just like that—*poof!*—they were this instant family that was supposed to live happily ever after.

He thought he could make it happen, just as he'd made this nursery happen. He was rich and powerful and he could bend reality to his will because his illusion was that he was in control of his own life.

He would hate her when she took that away from him.

He looked up at her and there was no missing it—the way his face relaxed into that peaceful smile. The way his eyes lit up when he caught her gaze. Even—oh, God—even the way he leaned down and pressed a tender kiss to the top of William's fuzzy little head.

She was shaking with want, with need, with the wish to make this fantasy reality. *I don't want to wake up*, she decided. *If this is a dream...*

She was in love with her boss, one of the richest, most powerful men in Chicago.

No, that wasn't true. It had been, once, but not anymore.

She was in love with Marcus, with a man who cared for a baby boy he didn't have to, who'd once almost run away to Germany just to be free. She was hopelessly in love with a man who used his power, his influence, to pull her up next to him, instead of lording it over her.

If only there wasn't a wedding or a reality television show. If only they could go on ignoring the rest of the world.

But they couldn't. She had to end this charade before it destroyed both of them. She couldn't go to the wedding with him and that was that.

"I think Liberty needs to cuddle a baby," Marcus said, half to her and half to William.

So she took the infant in her arms and sat in the finest rocker money could buy and tried to stop looking as if she'd been flattened by a semi.

She gazed down at the baby boy in her arms. William. Her William, her second chance to redeem her mother's greatest mistake. She hadn't been able to save her little brother, hadn't had the power or the money or the skills to keep that baby alive. He'd never been anything but a ghost of regret that haunted her. But here this baby was, just as alone and lost as William had been.

Except for Marcus, his guardian angel.

What would happen to William when she and Marcus ended? Would Marcus still invest this kind of money and time in the baby? She didn't want to think that he'd punish her by punishing William. The child was innocent.

But she couldn't risk that. She couldn't risk losing another William, not when she had the power to save him this time.

She looked up at Marcus, who was making good-natured small talk with Hazel about cribs and diapers and babies.

She hadn't wanted anything to change. She hadn't wanted to risk the comfortable life she'd made for herself. And if they hadn't found this tiny baby in a shoe box by the trash, maybe they would have gone on as they had, Marcus gently teasing her during their morning runs and Liberty working every Saturday and their worlds crossing only in safely defined ways.

But everything had changed.

And there was no going back.

Thirteen

Liberty paused at the top of the stairs, her hand on the railing that led down to the beach. She just stood there for a moment, her eyes fixed on some point way out in the ocean.

"Beautiful," she murmured, turning a strange smile in Marcus's direction.

"Yes," he agreed, slipping his arm around her waist and pulling her into a light hug. They needed to get going. They'd delayed arriving for the Beach Blanket Bingo party as long as they could. They were quickly becoming unfashionably late and that would create its own set of problems.

But he didn't want to ruin this moment. Liberty was framed by the bright blue sky and the deep blue ocean. The salty breeze whispered softly through the sands on the private beach on Catalina Island, blowing the strands of her hair around her neck. He wanted to bury his face against her and let those hairs play over his skin.

No, he didn't blame her for not hurrying down to the beach.

He looked down to where the party was in full swing. Even though it was only three in the afternoon and the sun wouldn't set for hours, the tiki torches burned bright and the bonfire was already going. Easily a hundred people were lounging in the sand, getting drinks from one of the two bars that had been set up on opposite sides of the beach, or sitting around the bonfire. From this safe distance, it looked like fun. But he knew better.

He gritted his teeth and said, "Are you ready?"

She turned a quick smile to him, but he didn't miss the glimmer of fear in her eyes. "There's no going back, is there?"

"We'll go down, make the bare minimum of polite greetings, and then we'll hit the water, okay?" He pointed to where a cabana had been set up close to the water. "See all the boards? I'll get you a paddle board and we'll be out on the waves in fifteen minutes—twenty, tops. And most people aren't out in the water. It'll be just us."

She took a deep breath. "I'm going to hold you to that," she said, tugging her cover-up down over her bottom before she started down the steps.

"You look great," he told her again. He'd been telling her that ever since they'd gotten on the plane early this morning because she'd been extremely nervous. She'd tried to hide it, but he'd seen right through her confident smiles and stiff shoulders.

She'd spent the plane ride with her hands glued to the armrest. She hadn't said much of anything when they'd landed in Los Angeles to refuel and she'd said even less when they'd taken off to fly to Catalina Island, where Lillibeth's wedding was being held on the private lands owned by the Wrigley family. Liberty had turned an unnatural shade of green when they'd landed on the tiny airstrip carved into the top of the highest point on Catalina four hours ago. He'd never seen a single person drink so much ginger ale at one time in his life.

"You're just saying that because I'm mildly terrified," she said in an almost normal joking tone.

"I'm not. You're gorgeous independent of your fear level."

They made it to the bottom of the stairs, where she waited for him. "Fifteen minutes," she murmured, linking her hand with his.

"You'll fit in," he promised.

But as they strolled down the beach, approaching the bonfire—complete with pig roasting on a spit—Liberty's apprehension began to affect him.

It only got worse when Lillibeth caught sight of them and waved. In the space of time it took for her to make her way over to them, he realized he should have listened to Liberty. He shouldn't have come. To hell with putting on a happy face and showing the world that Lillibeth hadn't actually trampled on his heart and, by extension, trampled on the Warren name.

He'd thought he'd been making an acceptable compromise with his parents by agreeing to come to this wedding, but now? With the woman who cheated on him and publicly humiliated him strolling toward him wearing nothing but a tiny little white string bikini and a whole lot of gold jewelry?

Bad idea. This wasn't saving face. This was rubbing his face in his failures.

"Marcus, darling!" she cooed, as if he were a toy poodle. "Where have you been? You're looking marvelous."

"Lillibeth," was all he got out before she was planting kisses on his cheeks. He shot a helpless look at Liberty, who rolled her eyes. "This is quite...something."

She slid her arm around his waist and leaned her head against his shoulder as if Liberty wasn't standing a foot away. "Isn't it? I wanted something private and intimate." The tips of her fingers brushed against the buttons on the front of his garish pink-and-blue Hawaiian shirt. "Somewhere we could all just relax and…see what happened."

Warning bells went off in Marcus's head—was she flirting with him? Was that even possible? The bride flirting with the man she sold out to the press the night before her own wedding?

But then again, this was Lillibeth. She had not proven herself to be the most trustworthy of significant others. Of course she could be flirting with him. He wondered if her groom knew—or cared.

In a panic, he looked at Liberty. She was outright glaring at Lillibeth. Well. At least they were all on the same page.

Lillibeth looked up at him, her limpid blue eyes composed into some variation of regret. "I'm so glad you came. I feel terrible about how it ended between us, you know. I hope that we can—" she lifted one of her smooth shoulders in a shrug and then, unbelievably, lifted on her toes and leaned toward him "—make amends."

"I don't think that's possible." Marcus removed Lillibeth's arms from around his waist and moved to Liberty's side. She looked as if she was going to erupt at any moment. He took her hand in his and squeezed it. "Lillibeth, this is my guest, Liberty Reese."

Lillibeth blinked in confusion, as if she couldn't believe he'd say no to her. "Wait—Reese?" When Lillibeth's eyes focused, they zeroed in on Liberty like a heat-seeking missile. "Ms. Reese? You brought your *secretary* to my wedding?"

"It's nice to see you again," Liberty said in the kind of voice that made it clear it was anything but nice. "And actually, I'm an executive assistant."

"Really, Marcus," Lillibeth said, her nostrils flaring in a most horselike manner, as if she'd stepped in something unpleasant.

Marcus felt Liberty tense but before a catfight could break out, the situation got a whole lot worse.

"Marcus!" a high-pitched voice called out over the beach. Marisa Warren, draped in a sheer caftan that was blindingly lime green, sauntered up to them, a cigarette in one hand and a drink in the other. "There you are, you naughty boy!"

"Mother," he said, turning his head so she could kiss him on the cheek. This was fine. This was going according to plan. They'd get this over with, and then he and Liberty could hit the water. "Where's Father?"

Marisa waved the hand with the cigarette dangerously close to his shirt. "Oh, he's around, I'm sure."

Translation: he was probably screwing around. Jesus, was this entire wedding party going to devolve into an orgy? What happens on a private island beach stays on a private island beach? He felt nauseous.

Marisa's gaze passed over Liberty, categorizing and dismissing her in the blink of an eye. "Dear," she said, dropping her voice to a more conspiratorial whisper that did nothing to prevent Liberty from hearing every word she said, "I was so hoping to see you with Emma Green. She's such a darling young woman…"

"Oh, I love Emma," Lillibeth added, smiling at Marisa. "She'd be great for Marcus, don't you think?" The two women shared a friendly smile.

Liberty's grip tightened on his hand to the point of pain. "No," Marcus said in a fierce whisper. "I'm here with Liberty."

"Your secretary?" Lillibeth said, trying to pull off an innocent tone and failing completely.

But it worked on Marisa—too well. Her gaze cut back to Liberty with renewed interest. "Your *what*?"

Marcus pried his fingers out of Liberty's grip and slipped his arm around her waist. "Mother, you know Liberty."

"What are you doing, Marcus?" Marisa hissed in a whisper, as if everyone else were listening in. Gone was the soft, delicate voice she used in public. Instead, her tone could cut glass. He knew the warning when he heard it, but he refused to buckle. "We agreed," she said, dropping her cigarette and digging her fingers into his upper arm, "that you were going to bring a suitable date to this event."

"Liberty is perfectly suitable." Lillibeth made a highly unladylike snorting noise. "She is my guest," he said, shaking his mother off. "I am a grown man, Mother. I can see whomever I want."

For a moment, her mask of social acceptability snapped back into place. "But, darling, what do you think can be gained from this?" she said, looking at Liberty as if she weren't a woman, but a thing. A bargaining chip.

He stared at his mother. "I thought I might try being happy. Isn't that enough?"

Marisa's face twisted into a mask of rage. "You are an embarrassment to the Warren name," she threatened as if he were still eighteen and a flight risk.

But he wasn't eighteen, not anymore. He was not afraid of her, of any of them. "You're doing a fine job of that yourself," he replied, pointedly looking at her glass.

Marisa's eyes blazed with righteous anger. "I am trying to protect you, *dear*."

And he was six again, holding his nanny's hand, and crying as he stood in front of his parents and told them about how the men in masks in the big black car had pulled up next to them on their way home from the park and pulled out guns and threatened to take them away the next time. How his nanny had yelled and scared the bad guys off. Marcus had asked if they were going to call the police because the police were the good guys who'd catch the bad guys.

That's when his parents had exchanged a look and said, "Dear, we can't risk the Warren name. We'll protect you."

And two days later, Miss Judy—the woman he'd spent most of his six years with—had been gone and Marcus had been very much alone.

All to protect the Warren name.

He was only dimly aware that he'd taken a step toward his mother, dimly aware that he'd dropped his arm from Liberty's waist. Marisa took a step back, her eyes widening in alarm.

"Protect me?" He barked out a harsh laugh. "Is that what you tell yourself so you can sleep at night? You don't care about me. You never have."

"That's not true!" Marisa gasped.

"Isn't it? You got rid of my nanny for protecting me. And Father—he made all those scholarship offers disappear. He made the offer from the German soccer teams disappear. How was *that* protecting me?"

"German soccer teams?" Lillibeth asked in genuine confusion.

Marisa shot Lillibeth a hard look. Lillibeth crossed her arms and took a step back, her head down. She may well cower before Marisa Warren, but Marcus wouldn't cower. Not anymore. "We are in public," Marisa said in a harsh whisper, her gaze darting around.

"That's all that matters, isn't it? What the public thinks. God, what an idiot I've been. To think, after all this time, I'd been telling myself that things would get better if I just did what you wanted. If I went to school where you wanted me to, if I started the company you wanted me to—if I slept with the women you wanted me to."

His mother gasped. "Marcus!"

"It never mattered, did it? No matter how hard I tried to be the perfect Warren, it was never enough. Well, I'm done pretending we're a happy family because we never have been and we never will be. You wanted me to marry her?"

he went on, jerking his chin back in Lillibeth's direction. "Why? So we could spend the rest of our lives making each other as miserable as you and Father make each other? *No.*"

"That's not why," Marisa said and this time, he heard a note of desperation in her voice. "Be reasonable, Marcus."

"Be reasonable?" He laughed again. Heads turned in their direction, but he didn't care. "You mean, do as you're told, Marcus—right?"

"That's not what I said. Please, Marcus," she begged, her eyes huge. "People will talk."

"Like Lillibeth talked to the press? She hurt me and yet you insisted I take her back, insisted I make amends—the only reason I'm here is because it was the lesser of the evils. Let them talk. They can't do any more damage than she's done, than you've done."

"Hey!" Lillibeth protested from somewhere behind where he now stood.

"Be quiet," Liberty snapped. "You sold your story. You sold him out."

"Funny coming from you," Lillibeth fired back. "Who the hell are you? Just a secretary trying to sleep your way to the top. You're nothing."

"That's executive assistant and I'm a hell of a lot more to him than you'll ever be."

Marcus felt a welling of pride for Liberty. She would not be cowed, either. But more than that, she was defending him. God, he loved that woman.

"Marcus, everything we've done was to protect you," his mother offered weakly. "You don't understand. We just wanted to keep you safe."

"No, you just wanted to control me. I'm nothing but a pawn to you. I'm not here for her," he said, jerking his thumb at Lillibeth. "I'm not here for you. I'm not here for Father and I'm sure as hell not here for the Warren family name.

I'm here with Liberty. Stay out of my life." He turned to Liberty. "You were right. Let's go."

"Marcus, you *will* stay," his mother demanded. "You came all this way—it would be a scandal."

He stopped and made eye contact with Liberty. "What do you want to do?" she asked in a soft voice.

Honestly? He didn't want to admit that his mother had a point. It wasn't a great point—but storming out of here less than ten minutes after he'd arrived would make people talk.

"Fine."

He took Liberty's hand and turned back to Lillibeth. "Congratulations on your nuptials," he said as he pulled Liberty after him. Without looking back, they walked down to the water's edge.

Liberty barely had time to kick off her shoes and tug her cover-up over her head before Marcus was hauling her into the water. They walked straight out into the waves, hand in hand, and they didn't stop until the water was at her chest and she was beginning to panic.

"I can't swim," she reminded him when a wave jumped up and smacked her in the chin.

"Here," he replied, turning and scooping her into his arms as if she weighed nothing.

She let him and the water carry her as she looped her arms around his neck. She rested her head against his shoulder as he turned and began to walk parallel to the beach.

They were silent until Marcus stopped. They had moved far past the actual beach—maybe a hundred yards from the last cabana. They were, as promised, completely alone on the edge of the ocean. The other guests who were in the water were so far away she couldn't hear them splashing in the water.

Confident they wouldn't be seen or heard, Liberty leaned

back to look up at Marcus. His face was drawn tight, but she couldn't tell if it was sorrow or anger. The two emotions blended together too completely to see where one left off and the other started.

What had he said about a nanny? Whatever it had been, it had hit a true nerve with his mother. Liberty wouldn't have thought she could ever feel anything for Marisa Warren, but in that moment, the older woman had looked her age, haggard and worried. She'd looked like a mother who truly did care for her son.

One thing was clear. Liberty wasn't the only one with secrets.

"The past is in the past," he said in a tight voice, his eyes focused on a point so far in the distance, she wasn't sure human eyes could actually see it. "That went well."

"Swimmingly," she agreed.

Marcus looked down at her, a small grin on his face. "You can't swim."

"And yet, here we are. I believe I was promised a paddle board or something," she added.

"Later." His grin faded. "You stood up for me."

"I just backed you up. Your flank was exposed." But then she thought of how Lillibeth had looked when she'd called Liberty a nothing—vicious and victorious. And that woman hadn't been wrong. Liberty was a nobody. No name, no family. And in this crowd—where a mother would throw her son under the bus for the sake of the family name—being a nobody who came from nobodies was a cardinal sin. Liberty would never be forgiven, no matter how industrious or smart or loyal she was.

It was bad enough that he was sticking his neck out for her with his mother, in front of all these people. She just couldn't bear the thought of him realizing how much of a nobody she really was.

God help her, she never should have let it get to this point, where Marcus Warren was cradling her in his arms in the Pacific Ocean.

But she hadn't been able to help herself. He cared for her and she was terribly afraid she might love him, and if that meant she might have to beat the hell out of a debutante bride, then so be it. And he didn't ask, so she didn't tell him.

"Thank you for standing with me. For being here with me. This is why I wanted you here, Liberty. Because I knew, deep down, that this was how it was going to go." He sighed heavily and looked out onto the ocean. "Because this is how it always goes and I need things to change—"

"Hello?" The voice boomed off from their left, interrupting Marcus.

Dammit! She wanted to hear what Marcus was about to say. Scowling, Liberty twisted in his arms to see Erik Jenner paddling toward them on a surfboard.

Jenner waved and Liberty couldn't help but note that he looked relieved to see them. "Are you two hiding over here?"

Yes, Liberty thought, frowning at him. Why did it have to be Jenner—someone who knew that she was Marcus's assistant?

She was in no mood to have to tell one of the most powerful real estate moguls in Chicago to shove off. But she would, dammit. Friend of Marcus's or no.

"Jenner," Marcus said, his voice dropping in register. And just like that, he was back to being Marcus Warren, Billionaire. "How are the waves?"

"Lousy. This whole beach is pretty subpar," Jenner said. His casual tone didn't match the way his eyes were darting between Marcus and Liberty.

She was still in his arms. And he was in no hurry to set her down.

"I thought she was going to get married in Hawaii," Jen-

ner went on after a moment's pause. "Better beaches there."
When Marcus didn't reply, Jenner leaned forward and addressed Liberty. "I'm Erik Jenner. We've met, right?"

"We have. Liberty Reese." Liberty reached over the surfboard to shake his hand.

Jenner's eyes went wide as he said, "Ah," in a long exhalation. "I didn't recognize you out of your suit." He shot Marcus a knowing look. "That certainly explains *that*."

Marcus's eyes narrowed in challenge. "Comments?"

"None," Jenner said quickly. "Who the hell am I to judge? But your mother—"

"No," Marcus interrupted. "Don't tell me. I'm sure she's having heart palpitations or something melodramatic. Hence we're all the way over here."

"Fair enough." Jenner looked from Liberty to Marcus again. "So."

"So," Marcus echoed.

Liberty floated in Marcus's arms. She didn't know what, if anything, she was supposed to say right now. Lillibeth and all her vitriol she could handle. But Jenner was a friend of Marcus's. Guy friendships were not Liberty's specialty.

Marcus was the one who broke the silence. "Listen, Jenner—do you still need an assistant?"

"I might," he said hesitantly. "Why?"

Liberty looked up at Marcus in surprise. "Why?"

Marcus looked down at her, his eyes full of tenderness. "Things have changed."

"Marcus," she said in a low voice, "what are you doing?"

"Trying to make sure your boss isn't taking advantage of you," he whispered back.

"I thought you told me you couldn't survive without her," Jenner said, his tone cautious.

Marcus grinned at Liberty. "I can't."

She saw then what he was doing and she loved him for it.

Anyone else might have tried to keep her closer—keep her in his office and his bed. Or anyone with as much money as Marcus had could have easily told her she could quit her job and stay at home and he'd pay for everything. And it would be tempting. To be his? To not have to worry about money, about security?

But that would mean that Liberty would be a kept woman—as long as he wanted to keep her. That would mean giving up everything she'd fought for to hope and pray a man would marry her and take her away from her life.

That would mean she would be no better than her mother, who refused to save herself on the off chance a prince might do it for her.

That's not who Liberty was. And, God bless him, even though Marcus didn't know about her mother and her princes and everything Liberty had done—every lie she'd told—to get where she was today, he knew that she would always need her job, always need the security it promised.

He didn't need to know about her past. He understood her anyway.

"I have a job open. It's not as an executive assistant, though. That position was filled. I need an office manager. More responsibility, more involvement in the business."

"I know someone," Marcus said, still grinning at her. "Great people skills, amazing at organization. A quick learner." Her cheeks flushed, but she couldn't help it. "She's got amazing recommendations, too. She's worked for the best."

Jenner snorted. "Man, you are *gone*."

In the distance, a gong sounded. An honest-to-God gong. Talk about pretentious wedding accessories. They all looked up the shoreline.

"Luau," Jenner said. "I guess that means we have to go back and eat a pig."

Hearing the note of resignation in his voice, Liberty

looked at him. Out here, in his swim trunks, sitting astride a surfboard, he didn't look like the real estate mogul who'd tried to woo her away from Marcus. He looked like a regular guy—attractive, yes, but there was something about him that gave her the impression he didn't want to be here any more than she or Marcus did.

"I guess we do," Marcus agreed. "Hey, can we borrow your board? I promised Liberty."

"I can't swim," she explained when Jenner looked at her. "I hope that's not a job requirement."

Both men laughed at that and some of the melancholy tension dissipated. "Sure." Jenner slid off the side. "But after we suffer through this, I'm coming back out. You guys are welcome to join me."

"You're not going to give me and Liberty any crap, are you?" Marcus asked, helping Liberty up onto the board.

Jenner let go and held up his hands in surrender, which made the board shift underneath Liberty. "I'm not your mother, man." Jenner looked back up the beach and added, "Someone in this crowd should get what they actually want."

"We all should." He looked at Liberty. "Ready?"

Ready? For what? To go back and face a mostly hostile crowd who thought of her as nothing more than a secretary who was trying to snag her boss right out from under their noses?

No, that wasn't right. Was she ready to go back and stand by Marcus's side, protecting his flank while he defended her right to exist? Was she ready to do what it took to protect him—to protect them? Even if that meant taking a position with Jenner's company?

"Yes," she said, trying to paddle without falling over the side of the board. "I am."

Fourteen

When they returned to shore, Lillibeth stayed well clear of them, which suited Marcus just fine. He and Liberty ate enough of the roast pig to be polite and then got boards of their own and headed back out into the ocean. There weren't really any decent waves here but, given how Liberty squealed as she rode out the smaller waves, Marcus knew this was all she could handle. He stayed within easy reach of her at all times, but she fell off her board only twice.

When dusk draped itself over them, he and Liberty sat on their boards, holding hands as the golden sun dropped below the surface of the waters. "And I thought sunrise over Lake Michigan was something," she said, her voice reverential.

"It's beautiful out here," he agreed, stroking his thumb over her knuckles. "I'm glad we came. It was worth it to share that with you."

She turned a smile back to him, but it faded with the last red streaks of light as she turned to look at the beach behind them. "I suppose we have to go in."

"We can stay out," he said because he really didn't want to go back in. Out here, floating in the ocean with Liberty by his side, he didn't have to deal with Lillibeth or his mother's guilt or anyone's side-eye glances.

But he knew that, sooner or later, they'd have to face the reality waiting for him back on the beach.

"Marcus," she said in that teasing tone, "may I remind you for the fortieth time today that I don't know how to swim? So being in the ocean after dark seems like a particularly bad idea?"

"Fortieth? Is that all?" He tried to grin, but he knew she was right.

"I've made it through a whole day of not drowning," she quipped. "I'd hate to ruin my streak at this point. Besides, it's getting colder."

Without realizing it, his gaze dropped to her chest. He could just make out the stiff peaks of her nipples straining against the wet fabric of her bikini top. Yeah, they could get out of the water—and skip the bonfire entirely. "Come on," he replied. "But we don't need to hang out. They're all just going to get drunk anyway. More drunk," he corrected himself.

"I'd rather be in the hut with you," she said, catching his eye and giving him a sly smile.

He laughed. He wouldn't necessarily call it a hut. It was a cabin—a rustic cabin. Three walls, a bed, a small bathroom and expansive views of the ocean—and that was it. There wasn't even a shower—that was up at the big house, where most of the wedding party and the less intrepid guests were staying, including his parents. The estate had a few of these small cabins scattered around, complete with thatched roofs and open views of the ocean.

And a sense of privacy. Their cabin was down a rocky path, maybe three hundred yards from the rest of the estate.

They made it to the shore without a problem and dropped off their boards. It didn't take long to see that he'd been right—the bartenders were still pouring and the DJ had started playing thumping club music.

He looked around. Trust-fund babies, hedge-fund managers, debutantes and minor celebrities, all partying together under the haze of the bonfire's smoke in an alcoholic daze. This was his crowd. These were his friends.

But were they? Had he ever been happy with them? Or had it just been a never-ending game of one-upmanship and drinking?

He and Liberty gathered up their things and began the long walk back to their hut. Tiki torches marked the path, so at least they weren't stumbling around in the dark.

Then a voice called out behind them. "Marcus?"

His mother.

He almost kept going. But Liberty was the one who stopped and turned back. And since she was holding his hand, he had little choice but to do the same.

His mother was still in her lime-green caftan. The shadows the torches were throwing over her face made her look older than he'd ever seen her before. It was almost like looking at a ghost of a woman he'd known in a previous life. "Yes?"

She didn't reply until she caught up to him. "Marcus, I have something I need to tell you."

"I'm sure you do. That doesn't mean I need to hear it. Come on, Liberty." He started to turn but his mother latched onto his arm.

"Don't you turn your back on me, young man. I am still your mother. And…and I owe you an apology."

That tripped him up, so much so that Marcus physically stumbled. "You what?"

Marisa stepped into him, touching his face with the palm of her hand. It was almost a tender gesture. But Marisa Warren didn't have a tender bone in her body. "You don't understand what your father and I have done to protect you."

He stiffened. He didn't want to do this, didn't want to deal with the guilt and the burden of being the one to carry on the Warren name—at all costs.

She went on. "That's our fault. Perhaps we did our jobs a little too well."

"Yes, of course. You were obviously Parents of the Year." He tried to turn again but she wasn't letting him go.

"I didn't realize you remembered that nanny," she said, halting him in his tracks for a second time. "I'd hoped you'd forgotten about her."

He stared down at her in shock. "Forgotten about Miss Judy? I was almost kidnapped and she's the one who saved me—not you, not Father. And what did you two do? You didn't call the cops. You didn't find out who was behind it. You got rid of her. And you left me all alone."

Beside him, Liberty gasped in shock.

"But, dear," his mother said in a pleading tone, "that's not what happened." She sighed heavily, as if the truth weighed on her. Marcus didn't buy her act for a minute. This was nothing but manipulation, pure and simple. "She was the one who organized the fake kidnapping."

Marcus recoiled in disbelief. Miss Judy? The one who'd given him baths and taken him to the park and read him stories at night? The woman who'd make a big bowl of popcorn so they could watch *The Brady Bunch* together? The one who'd loved him? "I don't—*what*?"

"Why do you think we fired her? She staged the whole thing."

"How…" He was so surprised that he couldn't even form the words. All he could see was the woman with the graying streaks in her hair and the warm smile on her face. "She wouldn't have. She cared about me!"

Marisa shook her head. "She might have. But desperation makes people do funny things. We had a private eye investigate what happened. Why would kidnappers be scared off by a woman screaming? It didn't make sense."

He reached out behind him for Liberty. When her hand slid into his and he felt her step closer to his side, the panic that was building in his body eased back enough that he could try to think again. "Why should I believe you? Because you've lied to me before. You've told me what you thought I needed to hear to get me to do what you wanted. Why is this different?"

His mother gave him a long look. "You should believe me because it's the truth. What do I stand to gain by telling you this? You're going to be very mad at me, I know. I just... I never realized that you hated us for that. I thought we'd made it clear that we were doing what was best for you."

"Yes, you made it quite clear that I was not to worry about it. That doesn't mean I was able to stop the nightmares."

A look of guilt stole over his mother's face. "She was in trouble. She needed money. The day after the attack, we got a ransom note—we were to pay a million dollars or next time, we wouldn't be so lucky. It was a scam—she'd get the money and look like the hero. I'm just sorry that she saw fit to use you as a means to an end."

Confusion rolled through him—that and anger. His whole life spent checking over his shoulder for vans—all for nothing. "Why are you just now telling me this? Why didn't you have her arrested? Why did you let me live my whole life thinking there were people out to get me?"

His mother took a step back. "You were a child," she said in a pleading tone. "What was I supposed to tell you? That the nanny you loved had put you directly in harm's way? That she'd arranged for her brother-in-law and his friends to don masks and use real guns to scare your father into giving them a million dollars?"

"Yes," he said through gritted teeth. "You should have been honest with me."

Marisa scoffed. "You wouldn't have understood then. We didn't want to subject you to the police, to a trial—and, yes, the publicity. You were six, Marcus. You would have forever been the boy whose nanny tried to kidnap him. People wouldn't have treated you like a Warren. They would have treated you like this thing to be pitied. No," she said decisively. "We did the right thing."

"You only cared about the Warren name." That's what he'd spent the past thirty years thinking—they loved the name and the power that went with it. Not him. Never him.

His mother looked incredulous. "Of course we did. Your father was involved in high-level negotiations with the Saudis for oil then and our first thought was that the negotiations had gone sour. We couldn't risk showing weakness."

"You let those people go because you wanted to save face for a *business deal*?" That he could believe. That was exactly what his father would do.

Unexpectedly, her expression turned dark. "We *ruined* those people for what they did to you. Their hands were not clean and we dug every single misdeed of theirs up. They went to jail for other reasons, but you can be damned sure they knew we had put them there. No one messes with a Warren."

Part of him wanted to believe her, wanted to believe that his parents had actually cared enough about his well-being to mete out punishment as they saw fit. And there was a time in his life when he might have bought everything she said, hook, line and sinker.

But he wasn't that naive little rich boy anymore. And this woman no longer held that power over his life. So he drew himself up to his full height and glared down at her. "And I'm just supposed to believe you? All those scholarships that Father made disappear? Was my life in mortal danger then, too?"

His mother waved those questions away as if they were mosquitoes. "Wanting to run off and play soccer? Do you know how embarrassed your father was?"

"Yes, I can clearly see how I've been nothing but a massive failure my entire life. Well, get used to disappointment, because I'm done. I always did everything you wanted—the schools, the girls, the company. Now I'm going to do what I want and I dare you to try to stop me."

"Oh, Marcus, please—you're being melodramatic." Anything sympathetic about his mother disappeared in the flickering light of the torches. "Do you not see what we did for you? You're one of the most powerful men in Chicago. You could run for office. You *can* do whatever you want. That's what we gave you. The world is yours."

Marcus heard a strangled-sounding noise and realized it had come from his own throat. "Run for office?"

"Now," his mother went on, as if she'd won and he'd lost and everything would go on as it had. "It's unfortunate that you decided to go public with your little affair, but at the very least, we're on a private island. This can be suppressed. No one needs to know you were dallying with your assistant." She straightened the collar on his shirt. "Nothing needs to change. You're still a Warren and that means something."

This was it. This was the rest of his life right here. His mother might claim that she had no ulterior motive telling her little story about his nanny, but he saw through that lie. She was trying to pull him in, trying to make him trust her.

"...Emma would be a perfect choice," his mother was

saying, as if Liberty were nothing more than set dressing. "From such a good family."

"No."

"No?" His mother paused. "Well, there are other options if Emma doesn't work for you."

"I'm with Liberty," he said.

"Yes, well, just keep it quiet," Marisa said impatiently. "That's what—"

"No," he insisted, louder this time. "No, Mother. You don't get to pick. You don't get to dictate my life anymore. I didn't want Lillibeth. I don't want Emma. For God's sake, I didn't want to come to this wedding and have to put on a good face all because it fits some twisted version of what the Warren name stands for." His mother opened her mouth, but Marcus cut her off. "I'm with Liberty. I'm not going to cheat on her and I'm not going to use her and I'm sure as hell not going to cast her aside because you think I can do better. I want her and I'm damned lucky that she wants me."

His mother glared at him. "You're being difficult, Marcus. Do you really think she—"

"She's the only person in my adult life who has cared about me. Not about what I could do for her, not about what I can buy her—but about me, Marcus. I want someone who's honest with me, who would never lie and cheat. I want the one thing money can't buy. I want her love. And if that means I'm not protecting the Warren name, then so be it."

His mother's eyes narrowed to slits; she looked like a snake on the verge of striking. No, she wasn't going to let him go that easily. "This is exactly why we didn't tell you about your stupid nanny. You always were a fool. You—"

"I," he interrupted, jerking his arm free from her grasp, "am going to do exactly what I want."

Lesser men had cowered before that look of intense

hatred. But Marcus would not give. "Are you, now?" It wasn't a question, but a threat.

No, she wasn't going to let him go at all, if she could help it. "I am. And if you try to interfere? I will do everything in my power to drag the Warren name through the mud. You think we lost face when Lillibeth sold me out? You have no idea how much damage I can inflict."

That got his mother's attention. Her eyes widened and she physically recoiled in horror. "You wouldn't *dare*."

"Try me and we'll find out."

They stood in a furious silence for a moment, trying to outglare each other. "I am very disappointed," his mother said softly, the simper back in her voice. "Very disappointed."

"So am I. God knows that when I have children, I won't treat them like pawns in some game that's rigged from the start." He turned, still holding Liberty's hand. "Goodbye, Mother. Don't look for me at the wedding tomorrow. I won't be there."

"Marcus?" Marisa called after him. "Marcus, this is not acceptable!"

But he didn't stop, he didn't try to figure out what twisted definition of love his parents had been using for the past thirty-some-odd years. Maybe they did love him and this was the only way they knew how to show it.

No, that was a cop-out because he'd grown up in that world, and even he knew that wasn't love. That was control. And he was done being their puppet.

Everything had changed.

And now he was free.

He began to run.

Fifteen

She had to tell him the truth. And she would, just as soon as he stopped sprinting along the dimly lit path—and pulling her with him. Liberty stumbled to keep up in her flip-flops. Somehow, she managed to keep her balance. But that was only physically.

Emotionally, she wasn't sure she'd ever find her balance again. How was she supposed to make sense of what she'd just heard? No, what his mother thought of her wasn't a huge shock. Nor was it shocking that what Marisa Warren had a problem with wasn't that Marcus was sleeping with Liberty, but that he'd gone public.

But... He'd almost been kidnapped as a kid? By his nanny? And his own parents—people who should have loved and protected him at all costs—had...well, she couldn't make sense of it. They'd put the perpetrators behind bars—but completely ignored Marcus while they did it? They'd kept him locked away from the world, as if it'd been *his* fault?

Her own mother had been a horrible person. Liberty knew that. Jackie Reese had been a sheep without a flock, lost in a hell of her own making. She'd ignored Liberty for drugs and men for years and years.

But no matter how bad it'd been—and Lord knew it had been pretty damn bad—Liberty had always had hope. She'd had Grandma Devlin teaching her to read. As shitty as the foster homes had been, the foster parents had fed her three squares a day and made her go to school. There had always been the promise that if Liberty put her head down and worked her ass off, she could save herself.

But Marcus—with all his money and all his power—had never had that hope. All she wanted to do was pull him into her arms and tell him it was going to be all right.

If only that were the worst of it.

But it wasn't because he really was going to fight for her. He really was going to risk everything—his name, his fortune—for her. He'd promised her that and he was going to keep his promise.

She'd tried to tell him that she wasn't good for him, that she'd hurt him. But he hadn't listened.

Well, that had to change, starting right now. She'd tell him about her childhood, about her times in foster care, about all those lies she lived with. He'd understand. After all, he understood how much she needed to make sure William was okay. It hadn't mattered to Marcus that William was a lost baby boy. Marcus would see that Liberty had done what she needed to in order to survive.

They crested the small hill in front of their cabin hut. He didn't even break stride as he ran up the single step that led inside. He only stopped when they reached the raised platform that held the bed.

Hands linked, they stood there for a short second, both of them panting from the run. His head was down and she knew he was hurting. And she knew telling him that she wasn't exactly the woman he thought she was would hurt him even more.

But she couldn't be yet another woman who lied to Marcus Warren. She was better than that. She had to be, if she wanted to be good enough for him. "Marcus," she began, trying to find the words. *I'm black—but I've been passing as white my entire adult life. My mother was an addict and a hooker. And I'm in love with you.*

"Don't talk," he said gruffly, turning and yanking her into his arms. Before she could react, his mouth crushed down onto hers.

It was not a tender kiss, not when his teeth clipped her lower lip. But she didn't pull away, didn't do anything but tilt her head to give him better access. She could taste the desperation on his lips—the confusion, the despair.

"Marcus," she said, pulling back enough that she could form the words. "I need to—"

"Don't want to talk." He jerked at the clasp of her bikini top and savagely pulled it off. The cold air hit her chest, still damp with ocean water, and she shivered when her nipples went tight. Then his mouth was against her bare skin, sucking her nipple into his mouth. "Let me take care of you."

"Marcus..." This wasn't about him taking care of her— she needed to take care of him. She needed to protect him. But his mouth was on her body and he was yanking down her bikini bottoms and sliding his hands up between her legs and...and she couldn't fight the rising surge of desire.

Still, she knew this wasn't about her. It wasn't. This was about him and dammit all, she needed to do something to tell him that she'd be here for him, however he needed her. "It's going to be okay," she said because that's what he needed to hear. Because that was what she'd always wanted to know when she was being thrown around by her mother's fate. She reached for his board shorts and began to pull them down. "Everything's going to be okay."

"Stop talking." He pushed her back down onto the bed and grabbed a condom. Before she'd even gotten his shorts all the way off, he spread her legs and plunged into her with a savageness that she'd never experienced before. She gasped as he filled her completely in one sure stroke, her body shuddering to take him in.

He paused, hovering over her, his head down. He was breathing hard, although she didn't know if that was from the sprint back to their hut or from the conversation with his mother or what.

"It's okay," she murmured. She ran her fingers through his hair, trying to lift his face so she could see him. They'd been lovers for only a week now and she was still getting used to the feeling of Marcus's body joined to hers. "It's okay, baby." She wasn't sure if she was telling him or herself.

She expected him to move   but she didn't expect him to grab her hands and hold them over her head. Then his mouth closed over hers again and he furiously kissed her as he began to thrust.

For the first time, she was completely at his mercy. He'd spent the past week making sure that she was comfortable, that she was okay with what was happening. Any sweetness was gone, however, as he drove into her harder and harder.

If it'd been anyone else, she might have been scared. But this was Marcus and she was his. She'd always been his.

But more than that, he was hers. This raw coupling, this furious need? This was how much he needed her. So instead of trying to reassure him, instead of struggling to get her hands loose so she could touch him, she gave herself over to him completely. This was what he needed and she could give it to him.

He shifted and held both of her wrists with one hand and then grabbed at her bare breast. He pinched her nipple with just enough pressure to make her gasp and, when she did, he covered her mouth with his.

He shifted again, slipping his free hand under her left leg and holding her thigh up so that he could thrust deeper. Electricity filled the air between them, making her skin prickle as her climax began to build. "Yes," she hissed at him. "Oh, yes, Marcus."

"Babe," he groaned, his teeth scraping over the sensitive skin at the base of her neck. Then he pushed back and reached down between her legs, his fingers finding the place where she needed him most.

He pressed and thrust into her, and Liberty couldn't control herself any more than she could control the storms. Her climax broke over her like a clap of thunder. Marcus thrust a few more times before he froze. Then, groaning, he fell forward onto her.

She pulled her arms free of his grasp and hugged him to her. She didn't say anything, though. She didn't need to. She just needed to be here for him.

They lay tangled together, breathing hard, for several minutes before Marcus leaned up on his elbows, a sheepish grin on his face. "Okay?"

"Okay," she agreed. "More than okay." Except she needed to tell him. And she hadn't yet.

Before she could get her mouth to form the words, Marcus said, "Before I had you, I didn't know I could fight back, babe. But I'm going to fight for you—for us. You and me and even William."

The mention of the baby shocked her out of her little speech about mothers and prison and foster care. "William?"

Marcus rolled over and pulled her up into his arms. "I think maybe we should try to apply for custody. Together."

She sat bolt upright. "We should *what*?"

His smile this time was more confident—the smile of a man who knew what he wanted and was used to getting it. This was, after all, Marcus Warren—and very few people said no to him. "I know I'm screwed up and I know my parents probably aren't done with me yet. But it doesn't matter what they think, what anyone thinks, I'm not going to hide you and I'm not going to let you go. I'm going to fight for you, Liberty." He touched her face, his fingertips trailing over her cheek. "I can give you anything you want. And you want William."

"But—I work. I *need* to work. And what about Jenner?"

"I know it bothers you to carry on an affair with your boss. I'm not that fond of the circumstances myself. My father is notorious for sleeping with his assistants, and I want to be better than that. I want us to be on a level playing field."

"But—the baby?"

He shrugged. "We can hire a nanny or you can take some time off. A year."

She stared at him openmouthed. "But…"

"There are no *but*s here, Liberty. I want you. I think I've known that for a long time. I want to wake up in the morning with you in my arms and I want you in my bed every night. You are the one person I trust and I can't imagine life without you anymore. Come live with me." He sat up and touched his head to hers. "Come be my family. You and me and William."

"Marcus…" *I'm black. My mother was a convict.* "You should know—"

He shook his head. "No, I don't want to know. Really, Liberty—it doesn't matter. I can't change your past any more than I can change mine. It doesn't matter any more than my mother's version of what my nanny did matters. It's over and done and I'm not looking over my shoulder anymore. I know what I need to know—that I love you and I want you," he whispered, his thumb stroking over her cheek.

She couldn't. She shouldn't.

Then he said, "Let me be your family, Liberty—that's what I want. Be my family. Be mine."

And how was she supposed to say no to that? If the life she'd been born into truly didn't matter to him, then it didn't matter to her. Jackie Reese was dead and gone, and so was her grubby little baby girl. The woman she was now—that was who mattered. She mattered because Marcus loved her.

"That's what I want, too," she told him.

He began to laugh, a happy noise that couldn't be stopped. And she laughed with him.

Because she wanted to.

Sixteen

"Why are we doing this again?" Liberty stopped in front of the nondescript building that held the offices for the producers of *Feeding Frenzy*.

It'd been two days since they'd left Catalina Island early Saturday morning—hours before the Hanson-Spears wedding had been scheduled to take place. Since then, they'd been ensconced in a suite at the Beverly Hills Hotel, feasting on room service and each other.

Marcus had no idea if Lillibeth had actually gotten married or what his mother had told people about their absence. And what was more, he didn't care. "We have a meeting. It would be rude to bail."

Liberty made a noise of frustration. "I didn't think meeting with reality-show producers was a good idea before we got involved," she said. "And now? I think it's a *really* bad idea."

"I'm not going to do the show," he said, holding her hand as they headed inside. The fact that she was arguing with him made him smile. He couldn't have this kind of honest conversation with anyone else. Just her.

"Then why meet with them at all? You don't have to do this."

"Look." He stopped and turned to face her. "My parents are insane."

"No argument here," she replied, wrinkling her nose.

"But," Marcus went on, "they're right—to a degree," he hastily added when Liberty rolled her eyes. "I do have a business image to maintain. So this isn't about building my brand name. This meeting is more about keeping investment options open. I'll listen to their pitch, politely say it's not for me and who knows? Maybe in a year or three, someone remembers this meeting and they reach out to me with an investment opportunity." He squeezed her hand, hoping she'd see that this was a good compromise. After all, it would be foolhardy to close the door on potential investments. That was his whole business. "I could make movies."

"You could do that anyway. You're Marcus Warren," she reminded him, trying to look stern. But he saw the way the corner of her mouth curved up into a tiny smile. "You can do whatever you want."

"Speaking of that," he murmured, pulling her in closer. "What do you want to do after this? We can see the sights or…" He pressed a kiss right underneath her ear and was rewarded when she shivered.

They'd get this meeting out of the way and then they'd take another day or two to do whatever Liberty wanted. And after that, they'd head back to Chicago and he'd start working on assembling the necessary paperwork to get custody of William.

Liberty would move in, of course. And if she didn't like his place, they'd get a new place, one that was theirs and not just his. And he'd have to get a ring. "Or we could fly to Vegas and get married."

Liberty jolted against him. "Marcus…" she said in a quiet voice. "Let's—let's get through this first."

He looked at her—was that reluctance in her voice? But she gave him a huge smile, as if maybe getting married was exactly what she was thinking, too. "Think about it—but no Beach Blanket Bingo. That's final."

She laughed and he laughed with her. This was right. This was his life on his terms.

They were shown into a conference room. Liberty sat beside Marcus, her tablet out. He smiled to himself as she slipped back into her role as executive assistant as if nothing had happened. The only thing that seemed different about her was the business suit he'd bought for her. Everything else was the same.

The show staff filed into the room. In general, they were all slightly rumpled looking. Rick Chabot, the producer of *Feeding Frenzy*, introduced himself and his coproducers, assistant producers and executive assistants—seriously, how many people were in this entourage?

Finally, all the hands were shaken and they all sat down, Marcus and Liberty at one end of the table, Chabot and his crew at the other. "Now," Chabot said in a different tone from the one he had just used to introduce half of Hollywood. Marcus shot Liberty a look, but all she did was shrug. Chabot was studying his own tablet. "Let's get down to business. You and Ms. Reese are a couple, is that correct?"

"Yes," Marcus said in what he hoped was a casual voice. He'd just spent five minutes introducing her as his assistant. Where the hell had this guy gotten that information?

"That's going to be a problem for *Feeding Frenzy*," Chabot went on, without bothering to look up. One of his group tapped his arm and tilted a screen in his direction.

Chabot nodded and continued. "Gotta be honest with you, Warren—part of your appeal is your availability. You're hot, you're rich—you've got to be single for this show. Someone with her background isn't going to send the right signals to our target viewers, especially not women."

"Excuse me? What background?" He looked at Liberty and was surprised to see that she'd turned a ghastly shade of green.

Chabot studied his tablet before turning a critical eye on Liberty. "Is this correct? Your mother was a convicted drug mule and hooker? She died of an overdose?"

A different person leaned over and pointed at the screen. "Is that a picture of Liberty with her mother? But is she...?" The producer turned the tablet around so that Marcus could see the photo of a young girl, clearly Liberty, standing in front of an apartment building with a gaunt-looking, light-skinned African American woman.

There was a moment of total silence. Marcus knew he needed to say something—it was completely unnecessary to blindside Liberty like this. And it was patently untrue.

Except...

Except Liberty wasn't denying it. She wasn't doing anything—maybe not even breathing. If everything Chabot had just said had been a lie, Liberty would have laughed it off. She wouldn't just be sitting there, looking as if she'd been shot.

Because it wasn't a lie, Marcus realized.

"Where are you getting your information?" Liberty managed to ask in a strangled voice.

"We received an email," Chabot said. "We vet all our candidates thoroughly so we followed up." For the first time, he looked up at Liberty. "It's not personal, you understand."

"No, of course not," she mumbled.

"Now—you have a child you gave up for adoption, is that correct?"

That got an immediate response out of her. "What? No."

Chabot scrolled. "A boy named William? Is that not correct?"

Marcus gaped at her. She couldn't possibly—could she have?

"I do not have a child," Liberty said firmly. "Your source is mistaken."

"We're selling a specific image here—wealthy, powerful," Chabot went on as though Marcus gave a flying rat's ass for what he was saying. "Now, if you two were already married, that might be one thing, but if we're going to take this to the next level…"

He said other things about image and selling, but Marcus didn't hear him. All he could do was stare at Liberty. She did not meet his gaze.

Her mother was African American? An addict? And a hooker? Why hadn't she told him? She couldn't possibly think that it mattered to him, could she? Or had there been another reason she'd kept that part of her hidden?

No, not even hidden. She'd lied to him. And for what? She had to realize that her race was a nonissue to him. But what would she have gained by making him think she was something she wasn't?

I'm not good for you. That's what she'd said, over and over. All those times she'd tried to convince him not to take her to the wedding? Not to do this stupid reality show?

Was this what she'd tried to tell him? Was *this* what he'd said didn't matter?

"…market share," Chabot was saying. "And you can be listed as a producer, of course."

He'd rather gouge out his eye with a rusty spoon. "Well," Marcus said, standing up before he quite knew what he was doing. Because this mattered. This history—he couldn't wrap his head around it. He'd thought…well, he'd thought wrong.

All he knew was that there was no way in hell he was doing anything that would take him to "the next level." He shuddered at the mere thought. What did that even mean? His face on lunch boxes? Did people even have lunch boxes anymore? He didn't know and he didn't want to find out. "We'll be in touch," he lied. Then he turned on his heel and walked right out of that crowded room.

He didn't know if Liberty followed him and he didn't wait around to find out. He didn't want to hear her excuses. He'd heard it all before—from his mother, from Lillibeth. From everyone who wanted a piece of the Warren name, the Warren fortune—but not him. Never him.

They all told him what they thought he needed to hear. To "protect" him. No doubt Liberty would say the same thing. She'd been trying to protect him from the truth—but why? So it could be used against him? Or had there been something more to it? Something sinister?

Idiot. That's what he was. A fool of the first-class order. Because people always wanted something from him. His money, his power, his body—but not him. Never just him. He'd thought Liberty was different. But was she? She'd pushed back against coming to the wedding with him, against this meeting—and she'd made it sound like it was because she was worried about him.

But he saw the truth. She'd been protecting herself and her secrets. How many more did she have? Was this just the tip of the iceberg?

There was always a cost. Everything was a transaction. And if you didn't gain something you lost.

God, he was tired of being the loser. And this time, it was no one's fault but his own.

He realized he was already outside. He didn't remember walking out of the conference room or down the hall.

"Marcus," Liberty said in a soft voice behind him that, yes, had a tinge of fear to it. He could hear her footfalls now as she hurried to catch up.

He kept going. He had a car around here somewhere, a car with a driver. The guy couldn't have gone far.

"Marcus, wait—please."

He didn't want to. He didn't want to give her another second of his time. But he didn't know where his car was and he had no idea where he was going. The confusion metastasized into rage. This was his fault—because he'd dared to be a real man with her.

He didn't feel as real anymore. "Why?" He turned on her. "Why, Liberty?"

She stood before him, her eyes painfully wide. She looked awful and the foolish part of his brain that hadn't gotten the message that she was not to be trusted, she was not safe—she was just like all the rest—wanted to pull her into his arms and tell her it was going to be all right.

It wasn't, though. So he did no such thing.

"I…" She swallowed, clutching her tablet to her chest. Her bag gaped open on her shoulder. She looked as if she'd run after him. Maybe she had. He didn't care. "I called for the car. He's coming right away."

"That's what you have to say? That's it?"

"I didn't—we should—" Her back stiffened. "Can we at least wait for the car? If I'm going to be humiliated for the second time in less than an hour, at least I'd like it to be in private."

"Oh, yes—sure. We wouldn't want any more public humiliations, would we?"

For a moment, he thought she was going to bend. Her

chin dropped and her shoulders hunched and she looked small and vulnerable.

Fine. Good. She could just look that way. It was a trick, a play on his feelings. Well, he'd show her. He'd stop having feelings. That was his mistake; he saw that now. He'd allowed himself to care about someone. Her. He should have learned his lesson after Lillibeth a little better.

But then Liberty rallied. She straightened up and glared at him. "Can we wait for the car, please? Or is it going to make you feel better to put me in my place with an audience?" She glanced around them with an exaggerated motion.

Yes, people were milling around. No one was paying them a lot of attention, though. "You know what? It's not. It's not going to make me feel any better. But how tender of you to pretend you care."

"I do care," she responded, the fire lighting in her eyes. "Don't you dare imply I don't."

The rage in his chest built, swirling back on itself like a hailstorm picking up speed. God dammit, he could do some damage right now. He could leave a wake of destruction in his path and watch the world burn.

"You're a fine one to be talking about daring. When were you going to tell me? Or were you going to wait until we'd adopted that baby? Until we had children of our own?"

"William is not my child." She paused, as if she was collecting herself. Or was she just trying to get her story straight? "He couldn't be. You were my first."

"You were a *virgin*?" he roared.

She flinched as if he'd slapped her. Heads around them turned. If people hadn't noticed them before, they sure as hell did now. "Marcus—the car—"

But the storm of rage kept on swirling and he couldn't fight it. "And you didn't feel like you should have mentioned that at some point?"

"I tried," she snapped. "I tried to tell you about all of it. You're the one who said the past was the past, and my past didn't matter any more than yours did. You're the one who cut me off. So, yes, I did feel like I should have mentioned it at many points. And I didn't because you didn't want me to."

"Because I thought you'd gotten your heart broken or you had to, I don't know, work your way through college—something common like that! I never imagined you were passing as white and hiding this! Because that seems important to me. I was going to marry you, for God's sake! I wanted to have a family with you! I trusted you with everything, Liberty. Everything. Things I've never told anyone else because I love you. And you didn't. You obviously didn't trust me at all."

"Marcus," she pleaded as tears started to drip down her cheeks. "I wanted to tell you but—"

"No. If you'd wanted to, you would have." Her tears were not going to move him. Not even a bit. "And you know what? It doesn't even matter. I don't care."

"You...don't?" Her chest hitched up as her eyes swam.

"An honest conversation, Liberty. That's all I wanted. That's what I thought I was having. I mean—is it all a lie? Did you even run?"

She flinched. "No. I never ran before I met you."

Everything he thought he knew about her was based on a lie. The past three years, their morning run together—that time had saved him. Because he had Lake Michigan and Liberty and the freedom to run, he'd been able to get past Lillibeth's betrayal. He'd been able to deal with the pressure his parents put on him.

He didn't think he'd be able to run his way out of this storm. "Nothing but lies. And why? Was it just so you could trick me into marrying you? So you could have a piece of the Warren name?"

That got a reaction out of her. "Don't be ridiculous, Marcus. I hate your name and I hate what your family has done to you because of it." The force of her anger pushed him back a step.

"Then why? And I want a real answer, Liberty. No more lies."

"Why? Have you ever tried being a black woman in this world? We aren't all born with a collection of silver spoons to choose from, Marcus."

He wasn't going to be relieved that she was fighting back, that he'd always loved how she argued with him when most everyone else would tell him what they thought he wanted to hear. The Liberty he'd loved had been a lie.

"Yes, my mother was black and yes, my father was probably white. I don't know. All I know is that passing meant I only had to work twice as hard to get out of the gutter instead of four times as hard. So yes, I passed. Yes, I let everyone think I was a middle-class white girl. I'm not about to apologize for what I had to do to survive."

"I don't want you to apologize for surviving, dammit."

"Then what do you want from me?"

"I wanted the *real* you, Liberty."

Her eyes flicked behind him. "The car is here. I'll be happy to tell you what it was like growing up with a hooker junkie for a mother and being bounced around from foster home to foster home—in the damned car, Marcus."

"No, I'm done. I'm *done*, Liberty. Do you realize that I risked everything for you? I stood up to my mother for you, I bailed on commitments for you—I would have done anything for you." His voice caught in his throat but he ignored that. "I would have fought for you, Liberty."

She looked at him with so much pity in her eyes that it made him physically nauseous. All his rage seemed to blow itself out and suddenly he was tired.

He'd wanted things to change and change they had. Why hadn't he considered the option that they might change for the worse?

Because it got worse when she stepped in closer to him and laid her palm against his cheek and, fool that he was, he let her. He should push her away and put her in her place and make sure she knew that no one screwed over a Warren. No one. "I didn't want you to fight for me," she said, her voice soft and gentle. "I wanted you to fight for yourself."

Her words hit him like a gut punch. What the hell was she talking about? Of course he fought for himself! He was Marcus Warren, dammit all!

But before he could tell her that, she turned and, head held high, walked off. He thought she was heading for the front gate, but he wasn't sure. "What are you doing?" he called after her.

"Take the car. I'll make my own way home."

"That's it?" For some reason, he didn't want to watch her walk away. It wasn't that he wanted her to stay—he didn't. He just…he wanted the last word. He wanted to do the walking, dammit.

She stopped and looked back at him and he was horrified to see she was crying again. "That's all there can be. We both know it. Maybe we always did."

"Sir?" Marcus started. The driver was standing next to him, looking deeply concerned. "Sir, would you like me to get the young lady?"

That's all there can be.

"Can you get me another car here within ten minutes?"

"Yes, sir."

Marcus nodded toward Liberty's retreating form. "Take her wherever she wants to go."

That's all there was.

And she was right, damn her. They both knew it.

Seventeen

If Liberty knew where her mother was buried, she'd go to the graveside. She had so many questions and for maybe the only time in her life, she felt as if her mother might have had some answers.

Or at least, one answer. Was this what Jackie Reese had felt like when her prince in polyester failed to rescue her?

Not that Liberty had wanted Marcus to rescue her. But for a few days—less than two weeks—he'd been her knight in shining armor, ready to take on all comers to defend her from the cruelties of the world.

Liberty didn't know where her mother was interred. For that matter, she didn't know where Grandma Devlin had been buried, either. Liberty had no connection to her childhood. She didn't see people from the projects. She didn't have any old friends who kept her up-to-date on the neighborhood gossip. Hell, there wasn't even a neighborhood anymore. Most of the Cabrini-Green projects had been leveled to make way for trendy new housing, the likes of which all her old neighbors would've never been able to afford. Maybe that was the point.

Her old life was so far removed from the person she'd willed herself to be that it didn't seem as if she could be both versions of Liberty Reese. And being Jackie Reese's daughter was not the better option.

So she'd stopped being Jackie's daughter. That hadn't been a chapter—it'd been a completely different book, one that was finished and done and had no other bearing on her life now. As Marcus had almost come to believe, the past was past.

Except it wasn't. Liberty would never be free of Jackie.

She hadn't lied to Marcus. Okay, well—she had maybe bent the truth. But that wasn't the real problem.

No, Liberty had lied to herself. She'd convinced herself that Jackie Reese's daughter didn't exist and, as such, wasn't important. That's what little Liberty had always felt like back then. Unimportant.

But the woman she'd become? That Liberty was *important*. She was valuable because she made herself valuable. She worked harder and longer than anyone else. She had saved herself. To hell with princes.

She had no prince. In fact, she had no one.

Well, almost no one. Two days after she'd walked away from Marcus Warren, she knocked on Hazel's door and waited. She should have called before she came, but she'd been afraid that Hazel might not have let her come over. The older woman still might not let her in, but Liberty was desperate. She knew that this William was not the same as the little brother who had died all those years ago, unwanted and unloved. But this baby, here and now, felt like her only living connection to a past she'd tried to bury.

"Yes? Oh, Ms. Reese!" Hazel's large eyes looked up at

her through her thick glasses. "I wasn't expecting you or Mr. Warren today." She peered around Liberty, looking for Marcus.

"Actually, he's not here," Liberty said. There. She'd managed to keep her voice surprisingly level. She could do this.

"Oh." Hazel gave her an odd look, but Liberty ignored it. "May I see William?"

"Of course, dear. Come in. Mind the door."

Liberty entered and followed Hazel up the steps. Tomorrow, she was going to go into Marcus's office after hours, when she knew he wouldn't be there, and clean out her desk. Then she was going to start applying for jobs. She wasn't even going to bother contacting Erik Jenner. That was too close to Marcus.

She was unemployed and starting over from scratch for the second time in her life. Which had led her to one unavoidable conclusion—this would be her last visit with William. She couldn't afford to let herself get any more attached to the child than she already was because she could not afford the child and if she did get a job, she didn't know where she'd wind up. It'd be for the best if she weren't in Chicago anymore. Too many versions of her past here.

"...Ms. Reese?"

Liberty shook herself out of her thoughts. Hazel was standing just inside the nursery, a look of concern on her face. "I'm sorry?"

"I asked if everything was all right." She peered at Liberty with owlish eyes. "With you and Mr. Warren."

Oh. That. "I don't..." But her words trailed off as she saw William rocking in the brand-new swinging chair that Marcus had bought just for him, and her chest felt as if it was going to collapse back into itself. The whole room was a giant reminder of how very much Marcus had cared—for William, for her.

This was going to hurt more than she'd thought it would.

She understood that he felt betrayed. She couldn't blame him for that. But what stung even more was that he'd promised to fight for her—and he hadn't. It hadn't mattered how valuable she'd made herself and it hadn't mattered how much she truly cared for him. All that had mattered was that she hadn't fully disclosed the most painful parts of her life.

"I don't think that Mr. Warren and I will be able to apply to adopt William," she said, plucking the infant out of the swing. William made a small mewling noise as Liberty tucked him against her chest. His tiny body was so warm, so fragile.

"Dear, I'm so sorry to hear that. You two... I had hoped..." Hazel's voice trailed off.

Yeah, they'd all hoped. Liberty sat down and stared at William's face, trying to commit every last detail to memory. She'd come so close to being able to hold on to this child—to being able to hold on to Liberty Reese. But she'd flown too close to the sun and what went up had to come back down. "I came to say goodbye." She said it more to the baby than to Hazel.

William blinked up at her, his tiny little mouth stretching out. She desperately wanted to think that he knew her now, that the sound of her voice or the smell of her skin was familiar to him. That, somehow, he'd remember there once had been a woman who loved him so much that she'd risked her safe, comfortable life for him.

And Marcus said she never risked anything.

"Will you take our picture together?" she asked, shifting to retrieve her phone. The company phone, with all the company communication on it. She'd have to bite the bullet and get her own phone after this. She couldn't keep Marcus's property. And the dresses—those would have to go back, too. Part of her wanted to return them herself or sell them—that money could carry her for months while she hit the job market.

But that would be another level of dishonesty. Marcus would assume that she'd been with him only for the money. As much as she was worried about her financial future, she couldn't bring herself to lower his opinion of her any more.

Hazel cleared her throat and took the phone. With some fussing, she managed to take a few pictures. "You belong together," she said, handing the phone back.

"I know." It was only after she'd said it that Liberty realized she didn't know whom Hazel was referring to— Liberty and William? Or Liberty and Marcus?

"Dear," Hazel began delicately. "It might be best—for the baby—if you kept visiting for as long as you're able."

"Really?" Oh, how Liberty wanted to believe that. But was Hazel telling her what she thought she needed to hear?

"Oh, yes. He knows you, you know. And he's still settling in after that rough start..." Hazel looked at her hopefully. "I know it can't be a permanent thing. When you're a foster mother, everything is in a constant state of change. Babies come and go, and all I can do is try to give them the best start I can. He's already lost his mother. They haven't found her, you know. I don't think it'd be good for the little angel to lose you so soon, too."

Liberty's throat started to close up. "I'm—" She had to pause and take a breath. "I'm going to be looking for a new job. I might have to move soon."

"I understand. But even for a few more weeks..." She looked at William and smiled. "They know when they're loved. Trust me, it makes such a difference later on."

Wasn't that the thing that had saved her? Grandma Devlin had loved her. She'd never been able to take Liberty in, but knowing the older woman was right down the hall with a cookie and a story and a hug—that she'd be there when Liberty left the foster homes—that was what had kept Liberty going throughout a hellacious childhood.

"All right," Liberty agreed, trying her hardest not to sob and doing a lousy job of it. "If you say so."

Hazel made satisfied noises and bustled off to get William a bottle. When Liberty and the baby were alone, she leaned down and whispered, "I love you, William. I always will."

He sighed against her cheek.

And Liberty let herself cry.

Marcus waited at the office the next day and the day after that, but Liberty did not show up. He took that to mean that she didn't intend to come back to work. Fine. Great. He needed a new assistant and that was inconvenient, but whatever. He'd work around it.

This did not explain why he left explicit instructions with the security guards to call him the moment she came back. She'd left all of her things, after all. She'd be back. And when she did finally show up...

Well, he'd know about it.

He didn't want to speak to her again. But when his phone rang at nine fifteen at night and Lester the security guard was on the other end, telling him that Liberty had entered the building, Marcus still hurried down to his car and took off for the office.

As he drove, he wondered what the hell he was doing. He didn't need to confront her. He'd pretty much said what he needed to say. He was just...making sure she didn't walk off with office supplies or change all the passwords out of spite. That was all.

She wasn't there. "You just missed her," Lester said, sounding sympathetic.

Marcus noticed that the older man wasn't meeting his gaze. "Is that a fact?"

"Yes, sir," Lester said. He had nothing else to add.

Marcus went up to the office anyway—just to be sure. Liberty's shower supplies were missing from the bathroom. Her area was as neat as a pin, as always—but the drawers were empty. He checked.

She was just…gone. It was almost as if she'd never even existed.

Then he saw it—her company phone sat on the corner of his desk and underneath it was a small white envelope with *Marcus* written in Liberty's neat hand across the front.

He didn't want to read it.

But that's exactly what he did.

Marcus,

I will never forgive myself for the pain I have caused you. This was never my plan. I didn't want things to change because I thought I had everything I needed. I was wrong about that, too.

I think it's best for me to move on. I won't take the job with Jenner, so you won't have to worry about explaining anything.

Please don't hold any of this against William. None of this was his doing. I just wanted something better for him than what I had.

I hope you figure out what you want and you fight for that. Not for me, not for your parents—for you, Marcus. If there's one thing life has taught me, it's that you have to save yourself. No one else is going to do it for you.

Thank you for everything. The last three years have been a gift I don't deserve.

Love,
Liberty

He picked up her phone. He didn't know why he remembered her password and he didn't know why he entered it.

The phone didn't open up on the home screen. Instead, it opened up on the last app that had been used, and Marcus wasn't ready for what he saw.

There was Liberty, looking as if she hadn't slept in days. She had William in her arms.

The sight of the two of them—it tore right through him. Because he'd spent the past two weeks allowing himself to think of a different life from the one he had. He'd pictured running in the morning with Liberty as they pushed the jogging stroller. And later, Saturdays at soccer parks and movies on the couch and silly songs and dancing around. Taking Liberty to bed at night and waking up with her in his arms in the morning.

He had everything he wanted, he told himself as he stared at that photo. He didn't need her. He didn't need kids. He absolutely did not need a big, happy family.

And what the hell was she talking about? He was Marcus Warren and that meant something. That's what his mother had said and she was right. She was…

Marcus froze, his heart suddenly pounding so hard he was afraid it would rip right out of his chest. *His mother.*

She and his father—they'd hired a private investigator who'd dug up enough dirt on his old nanny to put her and most of her family in jail.

She was very disappointed in him.

And suddenly, Liberty's past had appeared out of nowhere.

He grabbed his phone out of his pocket and, before he could think better of it, dialed his mother. "Marcus, darling," she cooed. "How are you? Are you all right? I've been so worried about you."

He didn't even have to ask the question—she'd already answered it. No one else knew that Liberty was gone.

But she knew. Of course she did. She—she and his father—had been behind the breakup.

There were, however, a few questions remaining. "How long have you known?"

There was an unnervingly long pause before Marisa Warren cleared her throat and said, "Known about what, darling?"

"About Liberty. About her past."

"Really, Marcus—you've got to be smarter about these things. Once you're settled down with the right kind of woman—"

"Answer the damned question, Mother. How long have you known about her?"

"Why, since you hired her, dear. You didn't really think I was going to let a nobody with no name and no family just ingratiate herself into your life without finding out something about her, did you?"

Why was he surprised? He shouldn't be. And he wasn't going to give his mother the satisfaction of thinking she'd one-upped him. "So let me get this straight—you dug up all the dirt you could find, or thought you could find—on my assistant and then sat on it for three years?"

His mother didn't reply.

Keeping his voice level was the hardest thing he'd ever done. But he wouldn't give her the satisfaction, dammit. "You've been waiting this whole time for the chance to use Liberty's past against her, haven't you? Not even against her. Against me. You sat on this information for three damned years because you knew you could use it to keep me in line, didn't you? *Didn't you?*"

So much for keeping his voice level. He didn't care. No one was around to hear him. He was completely alone because he'd fallen right into the trap without even realizing it had been set for him.

He'd done exactly what his mother wanted him to do. He'd pushed Liberty away.

"You're being ridiculous, Marcus. Think of what she could have cost you. And that baby? What were you think—"

He hung up. And when she called him right back, he turned his phone off.

Everything had a price and you either gained or you lost. That was the game he'd been raised to play. You gained favors and cashed them in when you needed them. Failure to do so meant you lost the game—you lost face, you lost business, you lost your name. Winners or losers, that's who made up the world, and Warrens were always winners. Always.

Except the game was a lie. He wasn't a player. He was a pawn. He was never supposed to win anything. He was nothing more than a favor to be accrued or cashed in. Everyone wanted something from him.

Except for Liberty. She hadn't asked him for anything. Not even a recommendation. And she would do anything for that baby. Including risking her job—and her heart.

If there's one thing life has taught me, it's that you have to save yourself. No one else is going to do it for you. That line from Liberty's note jumped out at him.

He hadn't thought he needed saving. He hadn't realized he had to fight for himself. He wasn't some helpless newborn. He had the ways and means to accomplish what he wanted.

But had he? Or had he just gone along with his parents to get by? He saw now what Liberty meant—what she'd always meant when she'd told him not to go to the wedding because he didn't want to, not to meet with the producers because he didn't want to.

All this time, she'd been telling him to fight for what he wanted.

He picked up her phone again and looked at the picture of Liberty and William. He loved her—he loved them both. What he'd wanted was a family. Liberty and William and more babies—one big happy family. His forever family.

He knew what he wanted.

Now he just had to fight for it.

No one was going to stand in his way this time.

Eighteen

"Ms. Reese? This is Trish Longmire of the One Child, One World charity."

"Hello," Liberty said, stopping in the middle of the sidewalk and fiddling with her new phone so that she could hear better. She had about two blocks to go before she got to Hazel's house. This was her third visit this week to feed and cuddle William.

She tried to think—had she applied at this organization? She'd sent out a lot of résumés, but she didn't recognize the name. The sun beat down on her head and she began to sweat. "How can I help you?"

"One Child provides basic school supplies to children living at or below the poverty line and grants to upgrade classroom technology at schools in need, primarily schools on reservations."

"A noble cause," Liberty said. Education had saved her from crushing poverty, after all. "But I have to ask—what does this have to do with me?"

"The Longmire Foundation has given us a considerable endowment and a mandate to get computers into classrooms."

The Longmire Foundation? That name she recognized— Nate Longmire was the Boy Billionaire of Silicon Valley who'd made headlines when he'd married a young woman no one had ever heard of from...

Oh, God. "I'm sorry—did you say Trish *Longmire*?"

Trish laughed. "Yes. We're expanding our efforts. I'd like to offer you the job of our urban outreach coordinator. You were highly recommended."

"But—who? I haven't applied for the job!" she said, her voice squeaking. Was this happening?

"Marcus Warren," Trish said, although Liberty should have guessed—who else could it be? "We need someone who's comfortable in both underprivileged classrooms, and organizing and attending fundraising events. I understand that you can personally attest to the value of a good education in changing your circumstances, but you've spent the last three years singlehandedly managing Warren Capital," Trish went on. "That makes you uniquely qualified."

"I—am?" Liberty cleared her throat. She needed to be making a better impression here. But she'd spent years— *years*—hiding her childhood. And this woman was telling her it was an asset? "I am, of course. Qualified, that is. I, um..." she babbled. "I'm sorry. This is quite unexpected."

"I understand. I'd like to fly you out to San Francisco next week so we can work out the details, if you're interested in the position."

"Of course. That would be—San Francisco. Yes!"

She and Trish exchanged emails, and then the call ended. Liberty sagged against the parking meter, staring at the screen of her new phone. What had just happened? Had Marcus really called up the wife of another billionaire and recommended Liberty? For a job? For which she was "uniquely qualified"?

She hadn't seen him since the blowup in the parking lot a week and a half ago. She hadn't heard from him, either—not so much as a peep. True, she hadn't exactly left her new number or anything but…

It was over. She'd kept the truth from him and he'd broken his promise to fight for her and that was that. That's all there could be.

Wasn't it?

On shaky legs, she managed to walk the rest of the way to Hazel's house. The shocks just kept right on coming, though, because Marcus's sleek Aston Martin was parked out front.

Oh, God. Marcus was here. Liberty was physically a hot mess—she'd sweat through the back of her tank top and her hair was frizzing. And Marcus was here. With William.

Oh, *God*.

But before she could bolt, the door swung open and there was Hazel, all big smiles. "Ah, Ms. Reese—Mr. Warren is waiting for you."

"He is? How did he know when I'd be here?"

"Oh," Hazel said, shooing her inside and waiting until Liberty hip checked the door shut, "he called shortly after your last visit." She scurried up the stairs with more energy than Liberty had ever seen out of her. "William is so glad to see him again—you can just tell."

Liberty stared at Hazel's back. Maybe none of this was real. Maybe she'd fallen getting off the bus and hit her head and was currently hallucinating. That would be almost as plausible as a job offer out of the blue and Marcus cuddling a happy William.

Stuck somewhere between panic and disbelief, she followed Hazel upstairs and into the nursery. What was Marcus doing here? What was he doing, period?

Oh. He was playing with a baby, that's what. Marcus Warren, one of the most powerful men in all of Chicago— if not the nation—was sitting on the floor of Hazel's nursery, making circles with William's legs and going "whee!" And William? He was kicking his little legs in what looked like sheer joy every time Marcus paused.

"She's here!" Hazel crowed in victory.

Marcus paused mid-*whee* and looked up at Liberty. "Hey, William," he said, carefully turning the infant around. "Look who's here."

William's legs kept right on kicking and his plump arms lifted in her direction. Hazel was right. William did know her.

"Marcus?" she managed to get out. "What did you do?"

That grin—that was the look he always got on his face when he didn't take no for an answer. And he was looking at her. When she didn't pick William up, he tucked the little boy against his chest and surged to his feet. "Hazel," he said, leaning around Liberty, "could you give us a moment?"

"Of course!" Hazel clapped—actually clapped—before she hurried to the kitchen. Liberty heard humming.

"Marcus," she said again, trying to sound stern. "What are you doing?"

The smile dimmed a bit. "Visiting William. Asking Hazel about what I need to do to apply for custody."

Liberty's mouth dropped open, but she quickly got it closed again. "Custody? Why would you do that?"

"Because I want to," he said simply.

"And—the charity? I just got a job offer—in San Francisco? What was that about?"

He shrugged, as if personally getting her a job was no big deal. "You need the work. I know you. I know you won't be happy if you don't have something to manage."

"But…why? Why did you do that for me? My past—you're done. We're done."

"About that." He shifted William in his arms and pressed a gentle kiss to the top of William's fuzzy little head. "I've been thinking about what happened and I owe you an apology."

She didn't even bother trying to get her mouth closed this time. "But—"

"No *but*s. Hear me out. Did you stop and wonder about how those producers knew so much about you? Do you remember Chabot saying they'd gotten an email?"

"I…guess? But so much happened—I didn't think…" But now that he mentioned it, that had seemed odd. "Who?"

"Well. It turns out that my mother had you investigated back when I first hired you and she'd been…saving these details, shall we say, until she could use them to her best advantage."

Liberty gasped, her hand against her chest. The violation was a physical thing, one that made breathing hard. Marisa Warren had known the whole time. "She *what*?"

There had been hundreds of opportunities for Marisa to use that information, too. She could have demanded that Liberty do what she wanted or she'd expose Liberty and all her little lies. But she hadn't. She'd waited for three years.

Marcus nodded grimly. "It was a lousy thing to do to you. You didn't deserve to be ambushed like that. She wouldn't deign to apologize, so I'll do it for her. I'm so sorry, Liberty."

"You're apologizing for her?"

William made a little noise and Marcus adjusted his hold on the baby. "And for myself. I should have listened to you—you were right. The whole weekend was a disaster and I…" He sighed. "I acted like a Warren. And that's not who I am. I want to be better for you. If you'll give me a second chance, I'll be better."

Liberty looked at the tiny baby, her second chance to make things right. "There's something else I should tell you, though, Marcus. The last time my mother went to prison—she went three times—and I was in my third foster home, she had a baby. He was born addicted to God only knows what. He didn't live past three weeks. I don't think he ever had a name. I never saw him. But I named him William because it was a good, strong name. Just like I named this baby."

"Is that all? Because if we're going to make this work, Liberty, I need you to be completely honest with me."

Were they going to make this work? Was that what he was doing here? For the first time, she began to hope this wasn't a dream. If this were really happening… "I don't like to run. But I do it anyway because I get to do it with you. Not at first—at first it was just because I needed a job. I needed to make myself valuable and if that's what it took, then that's what I did. I needed to be someone important, Marcus. And then, when I actually became that person, I couldn't untangle myself from all the little lies I'd told. I wanted to tell you, I did. But I was so afraid that if I did, you wouldn't look at me and see the woman I'd made myself into—all you'd see was Jackie Reese's daughter, and I didn't want to be that person ever again. I never did it to hurt you. I never tried to trick you. I tried to tell you. I just…"

He nodded, as if he truly did understand. "You just did it to survive."

"Yes," she agreed weakly. "I hope you can forgive me."

"Oh, babe," he said. Somehow, he'd gotten closer to her. With William cradled in one arm, he reached out and cupped her face. "Only if you can forgive me. That producer caught me off guard, but that doesn't excuse my actions. I made a promise to you—that I would fight for you, that I would protect you—and when the shit hit the fan, I didn't."

"You didn't," she said. She couldn't get her voice any higher than a whisper, though. Marcus Warren, the billionaire, was apologizing—to her. "You said it didn't matter, but it did."

No, that wasn't right. Because this was just Marcus. He was a little messed up, but he was a good and honorable man trying to make things right.

"It doesn't matter. Does knowing my nanny might have tried to kidnap me matter to you? Or the fact that I almost ran away to Germany—does that matter?"

"Of course not. That's not who you are now."

"Just like your mother's past isn't your present—or our future. I know I haven't earned your trust, but I'd like another chance." He slid his hand down her neck and pulled her in closer. "This time, I won't fail you."

Please don't let this be a dream. Or, if it was, Liberty didn't ever want to wake up. "But I'm a nobody. Why would you do that for me?"

"Because," he said, his lips curling up into a smile. He leaned down and, without squishing the baby, touched his forehead to hers. "The smartest, kindest woman I know told me to figure out what I wanted and go do it. Not because anyone else thought I should, but simply because that's what I want. So that's what I'm doing."

"But…me?" The baby sneezed and they both looked down at him. Liberty touched the top of his head with her hand. "And William?"

"I want you—both of you. I want to be a big happy family." He tilted her head back and stared down into her eyes.

"But you just got me a job in San Francisco."

That made him grin. "No, I recommended you for a job as an urban coordinator. They're branching out. As Nate explained to me, not all Native Americans live on reservations. And we happen to live in Chicago, which is urban. But even if you can't be based here, we could go together. We can start someplace new. I'll be happy anywhere—as long as I have you." He lowered his face to hers. He was going to kiss her, she realized—and she wouldn't have it any other way.

"I'm not good for you." She whispered the words against his lips. "I'll always be the daughter of a convicted criminal. People will always talk."

"Then be bad for me. None of that matters. What's important is you and me and what we know is true. Marry me, Liberty. Be my forever family. Let me prove that I'll never stop fighting for you—for us." He glanced down at William, who was watching this whole thing with big eyes. "For all of us. Right, buddy?"

William cooed.

"Oh, Marcus." Then there weren't any more words because she was kissing him and he was kissing her and they were trying not to squish the baby in between them.

"Is that a yes?" he asked.

"Yes." She lifted William from his arms and then leaned into Marcus as he pulled her against his chest. "*Yes.* I'm yours. I always have been."

"And you always will be."

* * * * *

NEVER TOO LATE

Brenda Jackson

Chapter 1

Twelve days and counting...

Pushing a lock of twisted hair that had fallen in her face behind her ear, Sienna Bradford, soon to become Sienna Davis once again, straightened her shoulders as she walked into the cabin she'd once shared with her husband—soon-to-be ex-husband.

She glanced around. Had it been just three years ago when Dane had brought her here for the first time? Three years ago when the two of them had sat there in front of the fireplace after making love, and planned their wedding? Promising that no matter what, their marriage would last forever? She took a deep breath knowing that for them, forever would end in twelve days in Judge Ratcliff's chambers.

Just thinking about it made her heart ache, but she decided it wouldn't help matters to have a pity party. What was done was done and things just hadn't worked out between her and Dane like they'd hoped. There was nothing

to do now but move on with her life. But first, according
to a letter her attorney had received from Dane's attorney
a few days ago, she had ten days to clear out any and all of
her belongings from the cabin, and the sooner she got the
task done, the better. Dane had agreed to let her keep the
condo if she returned full ownership of the cabin to him.
She'd had no problem with that, since he had owned it before they married.

Sienna crossed the room, shaking off the March chill.
According to forecasters, a snowstorm was headed toward
the Smoky Mountains within the next seventy-two hours,
which meant she had to hurry and pack up her stuff and take
the two-hour drive back to Charlotte. Once she got home
she intended to stay inside and curl up in bed with a good
book. Sienna smiled, thinking that a "do nothing" weekend
was just what she needed in her too frantic life.

Her smile faded when she considered that since starting
her own interior decorating business a year and a half ago,
she'd been extremely busy—and she had to admit that was
when her marital problems with Dane had begun.

Sienna took a couple of steps toward the bedroom to
begin packing her belongings when she heard the sound of
the door opening. Turning quickly, she suddenly remembered she had forgotten to lock the door. Not smart when
she was alone in a secluded cabin high up in the mountains,
and a long way from civilization.

A scream quickly died in her throat when the person who
walked in—standing a little over six feet with dark eyes,
close-cropped black hair, chestnut coloring and a medium
build—was none other than her soon-to-be ex.

From the glare on his face, she could tell he wasn't happy
to see her. But so what? She wasn't happy to see him, either,
and couldn't help wondering why he was there.

Before she could swallow the lump in her throat to ask,

he crossed his arms over his broad chest, intensified his glare and said in that too sexy voice she knew so well, "I thought that was your car parked outside, Sienna. What are you doing here?"

Chapter 2

Dane wet his suddenly dry lips and immediately decided he needed a beer. Lucky for him there was a six-pack in the refrigerator from the last time he'd come to the cabin. But he didn't intend on moving an inch until Sienna told him what she was doing there.

She was nervous, he could tell. Well, that was too friggin bad. She was the one who'd filed for the divorce—he hadn't. But since she had made it clear that she wanted him out of her life, he had no problem giving her what she wanted, even if the pain was practically killing him. But she'd never know that.

"What do you think I'm doing here?" she asked smartly, reclaiming his absolute attention.

"If I knew, I wouldn't have asked," he said, giving her the same unblinking stare. And to think that at one time he actually thought she was his whole world. At some point during their marriage she had changed and transitioned into quite a character—someone he was certain he didn't know anymore.

She met his gaze for a long, level moment before placing her hands on her hips. Doing so drew his attention to her body; a body he'd seen naked countless times, a body he knew as well as his own; a body he used to ease into during the heat of passion to receive pleasure so keen and satisfying, just thinking about it made him hard.

"The reason I'm here, Dane Bradford, is because your attorney sent mine this nasty little letter demanding that I remove my stuff within ten days, and this weekend was better than next weekend. However, no thanks to you, I still had to close the shop early to beat traffic and the bad weather."

He actually smiled at the thought of her having to do that. "And I bet it almost killed you to close your shop early. Heaven forbid. You probably had to cancel a couple of appointments. Something I could never get you to do for me."

Sienna rolled her eyes. They'd had this same argument over and over again and it all boiled down to the same thing. He thought her job meant more to her than he did because of all the time she'd put into it. But what really irked her with that accusation was that before she'd even entertained the idea of quitting her job and embarking on her own business, they had talked about it and what it would mean. She would have to work her butt off and network to build a new clientele; and then there would be time spent working on decorating proposals, spending long hours in many beautiful homes of the rich and famous. And he had understood and had been supportive…at least in the beginning.

But then he began complaining that she was spending too much time away from home, away from him. Things only got worse from there, and now she was a woman who had gotten married at twenty-four and was getting divorced at twenty-seven.

"Look, Dane, it's too late to look back, reflect and complain. In twelve days you'll be free of me and I'll be free of you. I'm sure there's a woman out there who has the time and patience to—"

"Now, that's a word you don't know the meaning of, Sienna," Dane interrupted. "*Patience.* You were always in a rush, and your tolerance level for the least little thing was zero. Yeah, I know I probably annoyed the hell out of you at times. But then there were times you annoyed me, as well. Neither of us is perfect."

Sienna let out a deep breath. "I never said I was perfect, Dane."

"No, but you sure as hell acted like you thought you were, didn't you?"

Chapter 3

Dane's question struck a nerve. Considering her background, how could he assume Sienna thought she was perfect? She had come from a dysfunctional family if ever there was one. Her mother hadn't loved her father, her father loved all women except her mother, and neither seemed to love their only child. Sienna had always combated lack of love with doing the right thing, thinking that if she did, her parents would eventually love her. It didn't work. But still, she had gone through high school and college being the good girl, thinking being good would eventually pay off and earn her the love she'd always craved.

In her mind, it had when she'd met Dane, the man least likely to fall in love with her. He was the son of the millionaire Bradfords who'd made money in land development. She hadn't been his family's choice and they made sure she knew it every chance they got. Whenever she was around them, they made her feel inadequate, like she didn't measure up to their society friends, and since she didn't come from a family with a prestigious background, she wasn't good enough for their son.

She bet they wished they'd never hired the company she'd been working for to decorate their home. That's how she and Dane had met. She'd been going over fabric swatches with his mother and he'd walked in after playing a game of tennis. The rest was history. But the question of the hour was: Had she been so busy trying to succeed the past year and a half, trying to be the perfect business owner, that she eventually alienated the one person who'd mattered most to her?

"Can't answer that. Can you?" Dane said, breaking into her thoughts. "Maybe that will give you something to think about twelve days from now when you put your John Hancock on the divorce papers. Now if you'll excuse me, I have something to do," he said, walking around her toward the bedroom.

"Wait. You never said why *you're* here!"

He stopped. The intensity of his gaze sent shivers of heat through her entire body. And it didn't help matters that he was wearing jeans and a dark brown leather bomber jacket that made him look sexy as hell…as usual. "I was here a couple of weekends ago and left something behind. I came to get it."

"Were you alone?" The words rushed out before she could hold them back and immediately she wanted to smack herself. The last thing she wanted was for him to think she cared…even if she did.

He hooked his thumbs in his jeans and continued to hold her gaze. "Would it matter to you if I weren't?"

She couldn't look at him, certain he would see her lie when she replied, "No, it wouldn't matter. What you do is none of my business."

"That's what I thought." And then he walked off toward the bedroom and closed the door.

Sienna frowned. That was another thing she didn't like about Dane. He never stayed around to finish one of their arguments. Thanks to her parents she was a pro at it, but Dane would always walk away after giving some smart parting remark that only made her that much more angry. He didn't know how to fight fair. He didn't know how to fight at all. He'd come from a family too dignified for such nonsense.

Moving toward the kitchen to see if there was anything of hers in there, Sienna happened to glance out the window.

"Oh, my God," she said, rushing over to the window. It was snowing already. No, it wasn't just snowing... There was a full-scale blizzard going on outside. What happened to the seventy-two-hour warning?

She heard Dane when he came out of the bedroom. He looked beyond her and out the window, uttering one hell of a curse word before quickly walking to the door, slinging it open and stepping outside.

In just that short period of time, everything was beginning to turn white. The last time they'd had a sudden snowstorm such as this had been a few years ago. It had been so bad the media had nicknamed it the "Beast from the East."

It seemed the Beast was back and it had turned downright spiteful. Not only was it acting ugly outside, it had placed Sienna in one hell of a predicament. She was stranded in a cabin in the Smoky Mountains with her soon-to-be ex. Things couldn't get any more bizarre than that.

Chapter 4

Moments later, when Dane stepped back into the cabin, slamming the door behind him, Sienna could tell he was so mad he could barely breathe.

"What's wrong, Dane? You being forced to cancel a date tonight?" she asked snidely. A part of her was still upset at the thought that he might have brought someone here a couple of weekends ago when they weren't officially divorced yet. The mere fact they had been separated for six months didn't count. She hadn't gone out with anyone. Indulging in a relationship with another man hadn't even crossed her mind.

He took a step toward her and she refused to back up. She was determined to maintain her ground and her composure, although the intense look in his eyes was causing crazy things to happen to her body, like it normally did whenever they were alone for any period of time. There may have been a number of things wrong with their marriage, but lack of sexual chemistry had never been one of them.

"Do you know what this means?" he asked, his voice shaking in anger.

She tilted her head to one side. "Other than I'm being forced to remain here with you for a couple of hours, no, I don't know what it means."

She saw his hands ball into fists at his sides and knew he was probably fighting the urge to strangle her. "We're not talking about hours, Sienna. Try days. Haven't you been listening to the weather reports?"

She glared at him. "Haven't you? I'm not here by myself."

"Yes, but I thought I could come up here and in ten minutes max get what I came for, and leave before the bad weather kicked in."

Sienna regretted that she hadn't been listening to the weather reports, at least not in detail. She'd known that a snowstorm was headed toward the mountains within seventy-two hours, which was why she'd thought, like Dane, that she had time to rush and get in and out before the nasty weather hit. Anything other than that, she was clueless. And what was he saying about them being up here for days instead of hours? "Yes, I did listen to the weather reports, but evidently I missed something."

He shook his head. "Evidently you missed a lot, if you think this storm is going to blow over in a couple of hours. According to forecasters, what you see isn't the worst of it, and because of that unusual cold front hovering about in the east, it may last for days."

She swallowed deeply. The thought of spending *days* alone in a cabin with Dane didn't sit well with her. "How many days are we talking about?"

"Try three or four."

She didn't want to try any at all, and as she continued to gaze into his eyes she saw a look of worry replace the anger in their dark depths. Then she knew what had him upset.

"Do we have enough food and supplies up here to hold us for three or four days?" she asked, as she began to nervously gnaw on her lower lip. The magnitude of the situation they were in was slowly dawning on her, and when he didn't answer immediately she knew they were in trouble.

Chapter 5

Dane saw the panic that suddenly lined Sienna's face. He wished he could say he didn't give a damn, but there was no way that he could. This woman would always matter to him whether she was married to him or not. From the moment he had walked into his father's study that day and their gazes had connected, he had known then, as miraculous at it had seemed, and without a word spoken between them, that he was meant to love her. And for a while he had convinced her of that, but not anymore. Evidently, at some point during their marriage, she began believing otherwise.

"Dane?"

He rubbed his hand down his face, trying to get his thoughts together. Given the situation they were in, he knew honesty was foremost. But then he'd always been honest with her, however, he doubted she could say the same for herself. "To answer your question, Sienna, I'm not sure. Usually I keep the place well stocked of everything, but like I said earlier, I was here a couple of weekends ago, and I used a lot of the supplies then."

He refused to tell her that in a way it had been her fault. Receiving those divorce papers had driven him here, to wallow in self-pity, vent out his anger and drink his pain away with a bottle of Johnny Walker Red. "I guess we need to go check things out," he said, trying not to get as worried as she was beginning to look.

He followed her into the kitchen, trying not to watch the sway of her hips as she walked in front of him. The hot, familiar sight of her in a pair of jeans and pullover sweater had him cursing under his breath and summoning up a quick remedy for the situation he found himself in. The thought of being stranded for any amount of time with Sienna wasn't good.

He stopped walking when she flung open the refrigerator. His six-pack of beer was still there, but little else. But then he wasn't studying the contents of the refrigerator as much as he was studying her. She was bent over, looking inside, but all he could think of was another time he had walked into this kitchen and found her in that same position, and wearing nothing more than his T-shirt that had barely covered her bottom. It hadn't taken much for him to go into a crazed fit of lust and quickly remove his pajama bottoms and take her right then and there, against the refrigerator, giving them both the orgasm of a lifetime.

"Thank goodness there are some eggs in here," she said, intruding on his heated thoughts down memory lane. "About half a dozen. And there's a loaf of bread that looks edible. There's some kind of meat in the freezer, but I'm not sure what it is, though. Looks like chicken."

She turned around and her pouty mouth tempted him to kiss it, devour it and make her moan. He watched her sigh deeply and then she gave him a not-so-hopeful gaze and said, "Our rations don't look good, Dane. What are we going to do?"

Chapter 6

Sienna's breath caught when the corners of Dane's mouth tilted in an irresistible smile. She'd seen the look before. She knew that smile and she also recognized that bulge pressing against his zipper. She frowned. "Don't even think it, Dane."

He leaned back against the kitchen counter. Hell, he wanted to do more than think it, he wanted to do it. But, of course, he would pretend he hadn't a clue as to what she was talking about. "What?"

Her frown deepened. "And don't act all innocent with me. I know what you were thinking."

A smile tugged deeper at Dane's lips knowing she probably did. There were some things a man couldn't hide and a rock-solid hard-on was one of them. He decided not to waste his time and hers pretending the chemistry between them was dead when they both knew it was still very much alive. "Don't ask me to apologize. It's not my fault you have so much sex appeal and my desire for you is automatic, even when we're headed for divorce court."

Dane saying the word *divorce* was a stark reminder that their life together, as they once knew it, would be over in twelve days. "Let's get back to important matters, Dane, like our survival. On a positive note, we might be able to make due if we cut back on meals, which may be hard for you with your ferocious appetite."

A wicked sounding chuckle poured from his throat. "Which one?"

Sienna swallowed as her pulse pounded in response to Dane's question. She was quickly reminded, although she wished there was some way she could forget, that her husband...or soon-to-be ex...did have two appetites. One was of a gastric nature and the other purely sexual. Thoughts of the purely sexual one had intense heat radiating all through her. Dane had devoured every inch of her body in ways she didn't even want to think about. Especially now.

She placed her hands on her hips knowing he was baiting her; really doing a hell of a lot more than that. He was stirring up feelings inside her that were making it hard for her to think straight. "Get serious, Dane."

"I am." He then came to stand in front of her. "Did you bring anything with you?"

She lifted a brow. "Anything like what?"

"Stuff to snack on. You're good for that. How you do it without gaining a pound is beyond me."

She shrugged, refusing to tell him that she used to work it off with all those in-bed, out-of-bed exercises they used to do. If he hadn't noticed then she wouldn't tell him that in six months without him in her bed, she had gained five pounds. "I might have a candy bar or two in the car."

He smiled. "That's all?"

She rolled her eyes upward. "Okay, okay, I might have a couple of bags of chips, too." She decided not to mention the three boxes of Girl Scout cookies that had been purchased that morning from a little girl standing in front of a grocery store.

"I hadn't planned to spend the night here, Dane. I had merely thought I could quickly pack things and leave."

He nodded. "Okay, I'll get the snacks from your car while I'm outside checking on some wood we'll need for the fire. The power is still on, but I can't see that lasting too much longer. I wished I would have gotten that generator fixed."

Her eyes widened in alarm. "You didn't?"

"No. So you might want to go around and gather up all the candles you can. And there should be a box of matches in one of these drawers."

"Okay."

Dane turned to leave. He then turned back around. She was nibbling on her bottom lip as he assumed she would be. "And stop worrying. We're going to make it."

When he walked out the room, Sienna leaned back against the closed refrigerator, thinking those were the exact words he'd said to her three years ago when he had asked her to marry him. Now she *was* worried because they didn't have a proved track record.

Chapter 7

After putting on the snow boots he kept at the cabin, Dane made his way out the doors, grateful for the time he wouldn't be in Sienna's presence. Being around her and still loving her like he did was hard. Even now he didn't know the reason for the divorce, other than what was noted in the papers he'd been served that day a few weeks ago. Irreconcilable differences...whatever the hell that was supposed to mean.

Sienna hadn't come to him so they could talk about any problems they were having. He had come home one day and she had moved out. He still was at a loss as to what could have been so wrong with their marriage that she could no longer see a future for them.

He would always recall that time as being the lowest point in his life. For days it was as if a part of him was missing. It had taken a while to finally pull himself together and realize she wasn't coming back no matter how many times he'd asked her to. And all it took was the receipt of that divorce petition to make him realize that Sienna wanted him out of her life, and actually believed that whatever issues kept them apart couldn't be resolved.

A little while later Dane had gathered more wood to put with the huge stack already on the back porch, glad that at least, if nothing else, they wouldn't freeze to death. The cabin was equipped with enough toiletries to hold them for at least a week, which was a good thing. And he hadn't wanted to break the news to Sienna that the meat in the freezer wasn't chicken, but deer meat that one of his clients had given him a couple of weeks ago after a hunting trip. It was good to eat, but he knew Sienna well enough to know she would have to be starving before she would consume any of it.

After rubbing his icy hands on his jeans, he stuck them into his pockets to keep them from freezing. Walking around the house, he strolled over to her car, opened the door and found the candy bars, chips and… Girl Scout cookies, he noted, lifting a brow. She hadn't mentioned them, and he saw they were her favorite kind, as well as his. He quickly recalled the first year they were married and how they shared the cookies as a midnight snack after making love. He couldn't help but smile as he remembered that night and others where they had spent time together, not just in bed but cooking in the kitchen, going to movies, concerts, parties, having picnics and just plain sitting around and talking for hours.

He suddenly realized that one of the things that had been missing from their marriage for a while was communication. When had they stopped talking? The first thought that grudgingly came to mind was when she'd begun bringing work home, letting it intrude on what had always been their time together. That's when they had begun living in separate worlds.

Dane breathed in deeply. He wanted to get back into Sienna's world and he definitely wanted her back in his. He didn't want a divorce. He wanted to keep his wife but he refused to resort to any type of manipulating, dominating or controlling tactics to do it. What he and Sienna needed was to use this weekend to keep it honest and talk openly about what had gone wrong with their marriage. They would go further by finding ways to resolve things. He still loved her and wanted to believe that deep down she still loved him.

There was only one way to find out.

Chapter 8

Sienna glanced around the room seeing all the lit candles and thinking just how romantic they made the cabin look. Taking a deep breath, she frowned in irritation, thinking that romance should be the last thing on her mind. Dane was her soon-to-be ex-husband. Whatever they once shared was over, done with, had come to a screeching end.

If only the memories weren't so strong...

She glanced out the window and saw him piling wood on the back porch. Never in her wildest dreams would she have thought her day would end up this way, with her and Dane being stranded together at the cabin—a place they always considered as their favorite getaway spot. During the first two years of their marriage, they would come here every chance they got, but in the past year she could recall them coming only once. Somewhere along the way she had stopped allowing them time even for this.

She sighed deeply, recalling how important it had been

to her at the beginning of their marriage for them to make time to talk about matters of interest, whether trivial or important. They had always been attuned to each other, and Dane had always been a good listener, which to her conveyed a sign of caring and respect. But the last couple of times they had tried to talk ended up with them snapping at each other, which only built bitterness and resentment.

The lights blinked and she knew they were about to go out. She was glad that she had taken the initiative to go into the kitchen and scramble up some eggs earlier. And she was inwardly grateful that if she had to get stranded in the cabin during a snowstorm that Dane was here with her. Heaven knows she would have been a basket case had she found herself up here alone.

The lights blinked again before finally going out, but the candles provided the cabin with plenty of light. Not sure if the temperatures outside would cause the pipes to freeze, she had run plenty of water in the bathtub and kitchen sink, and filled every empty jug with water for them to drink. She'd also found batteries to put in the radio so they could keep up with any reports on the weather.

"I saw the lights go out. Are you okay?"

Sienna turned around. Dane was leaning in the doorway with his hands stuck in the pockets of his jeans. The pose made him look incredibly sexy. "Yes, I'm okay. I was able to get the candles all lit and there are plenty more."

"That's good."

"Just in case the pipes freeze and we can't use the shower, I filled the bathtub up with water so we can take a bath that way." At his raised brow she quickly added, "Separately, of course. And I made sure I filled plenty of bottles of drinking water, too."

He nodded. "Sounds like you've been busy."

"So have you. I saw through the window when you put all that wood on the porch. It will probably come in handy."

He moved away from the door. "Yes, and with the electricity out I need to go ahead and get the fire started."

Sienna swallowed as she watched him walk toward her on his way to the fireplace, and not for the first time she thought about how remarkably handsome he was. He had that certain charisma that made women get hot all over just looking at him.

It suddenly occurred to her that he'd already got a fire started, and the way it was spreading through her was about to make her burst into flames.

Chapter 9

"You okay?" Dane asked Sienna as he walked toward her with a smile.

She nodded and cleared her throat. "Yes, why do you ask?"

"Because you're looking at me funny."

"Oh." She was vaguely aware of him walking past her to kneel in front of the fireplace. She turned and watched him, saw him move the wood around before taking a match and lighting it to start a fire. He was so good at kindling things, whether wood or the human body.

"If you like, I can make something for dinner," she decided to say, otherwise she would continue to stand there and say nothing while staring at him. It was hard trying to be normal in a rather awkward situation.

"What are our options?" he asked without looking around.

She chuckled. "An egg sandwich and tea. I made both earlier before the power went off."

He turned at that and his gaze caught hers. A smile crinkled his eyes. "Do I have a choice?"

"Not if you want to eat."

"What about those Girl Scout cookies I found in your car?"

Her eyes narrowed. "They're off-limits. You can have one of the candy bars, but the cookies are mine."

His mouth broke into a wide grin. "You have enough cookies to share, so stop being selfish."

He turned back around and she made a face at him behind his back. He was back to stoking the fire and her gaze went to his hands. Those hands used to be the givers of so much pleasure and almost ran neck and neck with his mouth…but not quite. His mouth was in a class by itself. But still, she could recall those same hands, gentle, provoking, moving all over her body; touching her everywhere and doing things to her that mere hands weren't suppose to do. However, she never had any complaints.

"Did you have any plans for tonight, Sienna?"

His words intruded into her heated thoughts. "No, why?"

"Just wondering. You thought I had a date tonight. What about you?"

She shrugged. "No. As far as I'm concerned, until we sign those final papers, I'm still legally married and wouldn't feel right going out with someone."

He turned around and locked his eyes with hers. "I know what you mean," he said. "I wouldn't feel right going out with someone else."

Heat seeped through her every pore with his words. "So you haven't been dating, either?"

"No."

There were a number of questions she wanted to ask him—how he spent his days, his nights, what his family thought of their pending divorce, what he thought of it, was he ready for it to be over for them to go their separate ways—but there was no way she could ask him any of those things. "I guess I'll go put dinner on the table."

He chuckled. "An egg sandwich and tea?"

"Yes." She turned to leave.

"Sienna?"

She turned back around. "Yes?"

"I don't like being stranded, but since I am, I'm glad it's with you."

For a moment she couldn't say anything, then she cleared her throat while backing up a couple of steps. "Ah, yeah right, same here." She backed up some more then said, "I'll go set out the food now." And then she turned and quickly left the room.

Chapter 10

Sienna glanced up when she heard Dane walk into the kitchen and smiled. "Your feast awaits you."

"Whoopee."

She laughed. "Hey, I know the feeling. I'm glad I had a nice lunch today in celebration. I took on a new client."

Dane came and joined her at the table. "Congratulations."

"Thank you."

She took a bite of her scrambled egg sandwich and a sip of her tea and then said, "It's been a long time since you seemed genuinely pleased with my accomplishments."

He glanced up after taking a sip of his own tea and stared at her for a moment. "I know and I'm sorry about that. It was hard being replaced by your work, Sienna."

She lifted her head and stared at him, met his gaze. She saw the tightness of his jaw and the firm set of his mouth. He actually believed that something could replace him with her and knowing that hit a raw and sensitive nerve. "My work never replaced you, Dane. Why did you begin feeling that way?"

Dane leaned back in his chair, tilted his head slightly. He was more than mildly surprised with her question. It was then he realized that she really didn't know. Hadn't a clue. This was the opportunity that he wanted; what he was hoping they would have. Now was the time to put aside anger, bitterness, foolish pride and whatever else was working at destroying their marriage. Now was the time for complete honesty. "You started missing dinner. Not once but twice, sometimes three times a week. Eventually, you stopped making excuses and didn't show up."

What he'd said was the truth. "But I was working and taking on new clients," she defended. "You said you would understand."

"And I did for a while and up to a point. But there is such a thing as common courtesy and mutual respect, Sienna. In the end I felt like I'd been thrown by the wayside, that you didn't care anymore about us, our love or our marriage."

She narrowed her eyes. "And why didn't you say something?"

"When? I was usually asleep when you got home and when I got up in the morning you were too sleepy to discuss anything. I invited you to lunch several times, but you couldn't fit me into your schedule."

"I had appointments."

"Yes, and I always felt because of it that your clients were more important."

"Still, I wished you would have let me know how you felt," she said, after taking another sip of tea.

"I did, several times. But you weren't listening."

She sighed deeply. "We used to know how to communicate."

"Yes, at one time we did, didn't we?" Dane said quietly. "But I'm also to blame for the failure of our marriage, our lack of communication. And then there were the problems you were having with my parents. When it came to you, I never hesitated letting my parents know when they were out of line and that I wouldn't put up with their treatment of you. But then I felt that at some point you needed to start believing that what they thought didn't matter and stand up to them.

"I honestly thought I was doing the right thing when I decided to just stay out of it and give you the chance to deal with them, to finally put them in their place. Instead, you let them erode away at your security and confidence to the point where you felt you had to prove you were worthy of them...and of me. That's what drove you to be so successful, wasn't it, Sienna? Feeling the need to prove something is what working all those long hours was all about, wasn't it?"

Chapter 11

Sienna quickly got up from the table and walked to the window. It was turning dark but she could clearly see that things hadn't let up. It was still snowing outside, worse than an hour before. She tried to concentrate on what was beyond that window and not on the question Dane had asked her.

"Sienna?"

Moments later she turned back around to face Dane, knowing he was waiting on her response. "What do you want me to say, Dane? Trust me, you don't want to get me started since you've always known how your family felt about me."

His brow furrowed sharply as he moved from the table to join her at the window, coming to stand directly in front of her. "And you've known it didn't matter one damn iota. Why would you let it continue to matter to you?"

She shook her head, tempted to bare her soul but fighting not to. "But you don't understand how important it was for your family to accept me, to love me."

Dane stepped closer, looked into eyes that were fighting to keep tears at bay.

"Wasn't my love enough, Sienna? I'd told you countless time that you didn't marry my family, you married me. I'm not proud of the fact that my parents think too highly of themselves and our family name at times, but I've constantly told you it didn't matter. Why can't you believe me?"

When she didn't say anything, he sighed deeply. "You've been around people with money before. Do all of them act like my parents?"

She thought of her best friend's family. The Steeles. "No."

"Then what should that tell you? They're my parents. I know that they aren't close to being perfect, but I love them."

"And I never wanted to do anything to make you stop loving them."

He reached up and touched her chin. "And that's what this is about, isn't it? Why you filed for a divorce. You thought that you could."

Sienna angrily wiped at a tear she couldn't contain any longer. "I didn't ever want you to have to choose."

Dane's heart ached. Evidently she didn't know just how much he loved her. "There wouldn't have been a choice to make. You're my wife. I love you. I will always love you. When we married, we became one."

He leaned down and brushed a kiss on her cheek, then several. He wanted to devour her mouth, deepen the kiss and escalate it to a level he needed it to be, but he couldn't. He wouldn't. What they needed was to talk, to communicate to try and fix whatever was wrong with their marriage. He pulled back. It was hard when he heard her soft sigh, her heated moan.

He gave in briefly to temptation and tipped her chin up, and placed a kiss on her lips. "There's plenty of hot water still left in the tank," he said softly, stroking her chin. "Go ahead and take a shower before it gets completely dark, and then I'll take one."

He continued to stroke her chin when he added, "Then what I want is for us to do something we should have done months ago, Sienna. I want us to sit down and talk. And I mean to really talk. Regain that level of communication we once had. And what I need to know more than anything is whether my love will ever be just enough for you."

Chapter 12

You're my wife. I love you. I will always love you. When we married, we became one.

Dane's words flowed through Sienna's mind as she stepped into the shower, causing a warm, fuzzy, glowing feeling to seep through her pores. Hope flared within her although she didn't want it to. She hadn't wanted to end her marriage, but when things had begun to get worse between her and Dane, she'd finally decided to take her in-laws' suggestion and get out of their son's life.

Even after three years of seeing how happy she and Dane were together, they still couldn't look beyond her past. They saw her as a nobody, a person who had married their son for his money. She had offered to sign a prenuptial before the wedding and Dane had scoffed at the suggestion, refusing to even draw one up. But still, his parents had made it known each time they saw her just how much they resented the marriage.

And no matter how many times Dane had stood up to them and had put them in their place regarding her, it would only be a matter of time before they resorted to their old ways again, though never in the presence of their son. Maybe Dane was right, and all she'd had to do was tell his parents off once and for all and that would be the end of it, but she never could find the courage to do it.

And what was so hilarious with the entire situation was that she had basically become a workaholic to become successful in her own right so they could see her as their son's equal in every way; and in trying to impress them she had alienated Dane to the point that eventually he would have gotten fed up and asked her for a divorce if she hadn't done so first.

After spending time under the spray of water, she stepped out of the shower, intent on making sure there was enough hot water left for Dane. She tried to put out of her mind the last time she had taken a shower in this stall, and how Dane had joined her in it.

Toweling off, she was grateful she still had some of her belongings at the cabin to sleep in. The last thing she needed was to parade around Dane half naked. Then they would never get any talking done.

She slipped into a T-shirt and a pair of sweatpants she found in one of the drawers. Dane wanted to talk. How could they have honest communication without getting into a discussion about his parents again? She crossed her arms, trying to ignore the chill she was beginning to feel in the air. In order to stay warm they would probably both have to sleep in front of the fireplace tonight. She didn't want to think about what the possibility of doing something like that meant.

While her cell phone still had life, she decided to let her best friend, Vanessa Steele, know that she wouldn't be returning to Charlotte tonight. Dane was right. Not everyone with money acted like his parents. The Steeles, owners of a huge manufacturing company in Charlotte, were just as wealthy as the Bradfords. But they were as down-to-earth as people could get, which proved that not everyone with a lot of money were snobs.

"Hello?"

"Van, it's Sienna."

"Sienna, I was just thinking about you. Did you make it back before that snowstorm hit?"

"No, I'm in the mountains, stranded."

"What! Do you want me to send my cousins to rescue you?"

Sienna smiled. Vanessa was talking about her four single male cousins, Chance, Sebastian, Morgan and Donovan Steele. Sienna had to admit that besides being handsome as sin, they were dependable to a fault. And of all people, she, Vanessa and Vanessa's two younger sisters, Taylor and Cheyenne, should know more than anyone since they had been notorious for getting into trouble while growing up and the brothers four had always been there to bail them out.

"No, I don't need your cousins to come and rescue me."

"What about Dane? You know how I feel about you divorcing him, Sienna. He's still legally your husband and I think I should let him know where you are and let him decide if he should—"

"Vanessa," Sienna interrupted. "You don't have to let Dane know anything. He's here, stranded with me."

Chapter 13

"How was your shower?" Dane asked Sienna when she returned to the living room a short while later.

"Great. Now it's your turn to indulge."

"Okay." Dane tried not to notice how the candlelight was flickering over Sienna's features, giving them an ethereal glow. He shoved his hands into the pockets of his jeans and for a long moment he stood there staring at her.

She lifted a brow. "What's wrong?"

"I was just thinking how incredibly beautiful you are."

Sienna breathed in deeply, trying to ignore the rush of sensations she felt from his words. "Thank you." Dane had always been a man who'd been free with his compliments. Being apart from him made her realize that was one of the things she missed, among many others.

"I'll be back in a little while," he said before leaving the room.

When he was gone, Sienna remembered the conversation

she'd had with Vanessa earlier. Her best friend saw her and Dane being stranded together on the mountain as a twist of fate that Sienna should use to her advantage. Vanessa further thought that for once, Sienna should stand up to the elder Bradfords and not struggle to prove herself to them. Dane had accepted her as she was and now it was time for her to be satisfied and happy with that; after all, she wasn't married to his parents.

A part of Sienna knew that Vanessa was right, but she had been seeking love from others for so long that she hadn't been able to accept that Dane's love was all the love she needed. Before her shower he had asked if his love was enough and now she knew that it was. It was past time for her to acknowledge that fact and to let him know it.

Dane stepped out the shower and began toweling off. The bathroom carried Sienna's scent and the honeysuckle fragrance of the shower gel she enjoyed using.

Given their situation, he really should be worried what they would be faced with if the weather didn't let up in a couple of days with the little bit of food they had. But for now the thought of being stranded here with Sienna overrode all his concerns about that. In his heart, he truly believed they would manage to get through any given situation. Now he had the task of convincing her of that.

He glanced down at his left hand and studied his wedding band. Two weeks ago when he had come here for his pity party, he had taken it off in anger and thrown it in a drawer. It was only when he had returned to Charlotte that he realized he'd left it here in the cabin. At first he had shrugged it off as having no significant meaning since he would be a divorced man in a month's time anyway, but every day he'd felt that a part of him was missing.

In addition to reminding him of Sienna's absence from his life, to Dane, his ring signified their love and the vows that they had made, and a part of him refused to give that up. That's what had driven him back here this weekend—to reclaim the one element of his marriage that he refused to part with yet. Something he felt was rightfully his.

It seemed his ring wasn't the only thing that was rightfully his that he would get the chance to reclaim. More than anything, he wanted his wife back.

Chapter 14

Dane walked into the living room and stopped in his tracks. Sienna sat in front of the fireplace, cross-legged, with a tray of cookies and two glasses of wine. He knew where the cookies had come from, but where the heck had she gotten the wine?

She must have heard him because she glanced over his way and smiled. At that moment he thought she was even more breathtaking than a rose in winter. She licked her lips and immediately he thought she was even more tempting than any decadent dessert.

He cleared his throat. "Where did the wine come from?"

She licked her lips again and his body responded in an unquestionable way. He hoped the candlelight was hiding the physical effect she was having on him. "I found it in one of the kitchen cabinets. I think it's the bottle that was left when we came here to celebrate our first anniversary."

His thoughts immediately remembered that weekend. She had packed a selection of sexy lingerie and he had enjoyed removing each and every piece. She had also given him, among other things, a beautiful gold watch with the inscription engraved, *The Great Dane*. He, in turn, had given her a lover's bracelet, which was similar to a diamond tennis bracelet except that each letter of her name was etched in six of the stones.

He could still remember the single tear that had fallen from her eye when he had placed it on her wrist. That had been a special time for them, memories he would always cherish. That knowledge tightened the love that surrounded his heart. More than anything, he was determined that they settle things this weekend. He needed to make her see that he was hers and she was his. For always.

His lips creased into a smile. "I see you've decided to share the cookies, after all," he said, crossing the room to her.

She chuckled as he dropped down on the floor beside her. "Either that or run the risk of you getting up during the night and eating them all." The firelight danced through the twists on her head, highlighting the medium brown coiled strands with golden flecks. He absolutely loved the natural looking hairstyle on her.

He lifted a dark brow. "Eating them all? Three boxes?"

Her smile grew soft. "Hey, you've been known to overindulge a few times."

He paused as heated memories consumed him, reminding him of those times he had overindulged, especially when it came to making love to her. He recalled one weekend they had gone at it almost nonstop. If she hadn't been on the pill there was no doubt in his mind that that single weekend would have made him a daddy. A very proud one, at that.

She handed him a glass of wine. "May I propose a toast?"

His smile widened. "To what?"

"The return of the Beast from the East."

He switched his gaze from her to glance out the window. Even in the dark he could see the white flecks coming down in droves. He looked back at her and cocked a brow. "We have a reason to celebrate this bad weather?"

She stared at him for a long moment, then said quietly, "Yes. The Beast is the reason we're stranded here together, and even with our low rations of food, I can't think of any other place I'd rather be...than here alone with you."

Chapter 15

Dane stared at Sienna and the intensity of that gaze made her entire body tingle, her nerve endings steam. It was pretty much like the day they'd met, when he'd walked into his father's study. She had looked up, their gazes had connected and the seriousness in the dark irises that had locked with hers had changed her life forever. She had fallen in love with him then and there.

Dane didn't say anything for a long moment as he continued to look at her, and then he lifted his wineglass and said huskily, "To the Beast…who brought me Beauty."

His words were like a sensuous stroke down her spine, and the void feeling she'd had during the past few months was slowly fading away. After the toast was made and they had both taken sips of their wine, Dane placed his glass aside and then relieved her of hers. He then slowly leaned forward and captured her mouth, tasting the wine, relishing her delectable flavor. How had she gone without this for six months? How had she survived? she wondered as his tongue devoured hers, battering deep in the heat of her mouth, licking and sucking as he wove his tongue in and out between teeth, gum and whatever wanted to serve as a barrier.

He suddenly pulled back and stared at her. A smile touched the corners of his lips. "I could keep going and going, but before we go any further we need to talk, determine what brought us to this point so it won't ever be allowed to happen again. I don't want us to ever let anything or anyone have power, more control over the vows we made three years ago."

Sienna nodded, thinking the way the firelight was dancing over his dark skin was sending an erotic frisson up her spine. "All right."

He stood. "I'll be right back."

Sienna lifted a brow, wondering where he was going and watched as he crossed the room to open the desk drawer. Like her, he had changed into a T-shirt and a pair of sweats, and as she watched him she found it difficult to breathe. He moved in such a manly way, each movement a display of fine muscles and limbs and how they worked together in graceful coordination, perfect precision. Watching him only knocked her hormones out of whack.

He returned moments later with pens and paper in hand. There was a serious expression on his face when he handed her a sheet of paper and a pen and kept the same for himself. "I want us to write down all the things we feel went wrong with our marriage, being honest to include everything. And then we'll discuss them."

She looked down at the pen and paper and then back at him. "You want me to write them down?"

"Yes, and I'll do the same."

Sienna nodded and watched as he began writing on his paper, wondering what he was jotting down. She leaned back and sighed, wondering if she could air their dirty laundry on paper, but it seemed he had no such qualms. Most couples sought the helpful guidance of marriage counselors when they found themselves in similar situations, but she hadn't given them that chance. But at this point, she would do anything to save her marriage.

So she began writing, being honest with herself and with him.

Chapter 16

Dane finished writing and glanced over at Sienna. She was still at it and had a serious expression on her features. He studied the contours of her face and his gaze dropped to her neck, and he noticed the thin gold chain. She was still wearing the heart pendant he'd given her as a wedding gift.

Deep down, Dane believed this little assignment was what they needed as the first step in repairing what had gone wrong in their marriage. Having things written down would make it easier to stay focused and not go off on a tangent. And it made one less likely to give in to the power of the mind, the wills and emotions. He wanted them to concentrate on those destructive elements and forces that had eroded away at what should have been a strong relationship.

She glanced up and met his gaze as she put the pen aside. She gave him a wry smile. "Okay, that's it."

He reached out and took her hand in his, tightening his hold on it when he saw a look of uncertainty on her face. "All right, what do you have?"

She gave him a sheepish grimace. "How about you going first?"

He gently squeezed her hand. "How about if we go together? I'll start off and then we'll alternate."

She nodded. "What if we have the same ones?"

"That will be okay. We'll talk about all of them." He picked up his piece of paper.

"First on my list is communication."

Sienna smiled ruefully. "It's first on mine, too. And I agree that we need to talk more, without arguing, not that you argued. I think you would hold stuff in when I made you upset instead of getting it out and speaking your mind."

Dane stared at her for a moment, then a smile touched his lips. "You're right, you know. I always had to plug in the last word and I did it because I knew it would piss you off."

"Well, stop doing it."

He grinned. "Okay. The next time I'll hang around for us to talk through things. But then you're going to have to make sure that you're available when we need to talk. You can't let anything, not even your job, get in the way of us communicating."

"Okay, I agree."

"Now, what's next on your list?" he asked.

She looked up at him and smiled. "Patience. I know you said that I don't have patience, but neither do you. But you used to."

Dane shook his head. "Yeah, I lost my patience when you did. I thought to myself, why should I be patient with you when you weren't doing the same with me? Sometimes I think you thought I enjoyed knowing you had a bad day or didn't make a sale, and that wasn't it at all. At some point what was suddenly important to you wasn't important to me anymore."

"And because of it, we both became detached," Sienna said softly.

"Yes, we did." He reached out and lifted her chin. "I promise to do a better job of being patient, Sienna."

"So will I, Dane."

They alternated, going down the list. They had a number of the same things on both lists and they discussed everything in detail, acknowledging their faults and what they could have done to make things better. They also discussed what they would do in the future to strengthen their marriage.

"That's all I have on my list," Dane said a while later. "Do you have anything else?"

Sienna's finger glided over her list. For a short while she thought about pretending she didn't have anything else, but they had agreed to be completely honest. They had definitely done so when they had discussed her spending more time at work than at home.

"So what's the last thing on your list, Sienna? What do you see as one of the things that went wrong with our marriage?"

She lifted her chin and met his gaze and said, "My inability to stand up to your parents."

He looked at her with deep, dark eyes. "Okay, then. Let's talk about that."

Chapter 17

Dane waited patiently for Sienna to begin talking and gently rubbed the backside of her hand while doing so. He'd known the issue of his parents had always been a challenge to her. Over the years, he had tried to make her see that how the elder Bradfords felt didn't matter. What he failed to realize, accept and understand was that it *did* matter...to her.

She had grown up in a family without love for so long that when they married, she not only sought his love, but that of his family. Being accepted meant a lot to her, and her expectations of the Bradfords, given how they operated and their family history, were too high.

They weren't a close-knit bunch, never had been and never would be. His parents had allowed their own parents to decide their future, including who they married. When they had come of age, arranged marriages were the norm within the Bradfords' circle. His father had once confided to him one night after indulging in too many drinks that his mother had not been his choice for a wife. That hadn't surprised Dane, nor had it bothered him, since he would bet that his father probably hadn't been his mother's choice of a husband, either.

"I don't want to rehash the past, Dane," Sienna finally said softly, looking at the blaze in the fireplace instead of at him. "But something you said earlier tonight has made me think about a lot of things. You love your parents, but you've never hesitated in letting them know when you felt they were wrong, nor have you put up with their crap when it came to me."

She switched her gaze from the fire to him. "The problem is that *I* put up with their crap when it came to me. And you were right. I thought I had to actually prove something to them, show them I was worthy of you and your love. And I've spent the better part of a year and a half doing that and all it did was bring me closer and closer to losing you. I'm sure they've been walking around with big smiles on their faces since you got the divorce petition. But I refuse to let them be happy at my expense and my own heartbreak."

She scooted closer to Dane and splayed her hands against his chest. "It's time I became more assertive with your parents, Dane. Because it's not about them—it's about us. I refuse to let them make me feel unworthy any longer, because I am worthy to be loved by you. I don't have anything to prove. They either accept me as I am or not at all. The only person who matters anymore is you."

With his gaze holding hers, Dane lifted one of her hands off his chest and brought it to his lips, and placed a kiss on the palm. "I'm glad you've finally come to realize that, Sienna. And I wholeheartedly understand and agree. I was made to love you, and if my parents never accept that then it's their loss, not ours."

Tears constricted Sienna's throat and she swallowed deeply before she could find her voice to say, "I love you, Dane. I don't want the divorce. I never did. I want to belong to you and I want you to belong to me. I just want to make you happy."

"And I love you, too, Sienna, and I don't want the divorce, either. My life will be nothing without you being a part of it. I love you so much and I've missed you."

And with his heart pounding hard in his chest, he leaned over and captured her lips, intent on showing her just what he meant.

Chapter 18

This is homecoming, Sienna thought as she was quickly consumed by the hungry onslaught of Dane's kiss. All the hurt and anger she'd felt for six months was being replaced by passion of the most heated kind. All she could think about was the desire she was feeling being back in the arms of the man she loved and who loved her.

This was the type of communication she'd always loved, where she could share her thoughts, feelings and desires with Dane without uttering a single word. It was where their deepest emotions and what was in their inner hearts spoke for them, expressing things so eloquently and not leaving any room for misunderstandings.

He pulled back slightly, his lips hovering within inches of hers. He reached out and caressed her cheek, and as if she needed his taste again, her lips automatically parted. A slow, sensual acknowledgement of understanding tilted the corners of his mouth into a smile. Then he leaned closer and kissed her again, longer and harder, and the only thing she could do was to wrap her arms around him and silently thank God for reuniting her with this very special man.

Dane was hungry for the taste of his wife and at that moment, as his heart continued to pound relentlessly in his chest, he knew he had to make love to her, to show her in every way what she meant to him, had always meant to him and would always mean to him.

He pulled back slightly and the moisture that was left on her lips made his stomach clench. He leaned forward and licked them dry, or tried to, but her scent was driving him to do more. "Please let me make love to you, Sienna," he whispered, leaning down and resting his forehead against hers.

She leaned back and cupped his chin with her hand. "Oh, yes. I want you to make love to me, Dane. I've missed being with you so much I ache."

"Oh, baby, I love you." He pulled her closer, murmured the words in her twisted locks, kissed her cheek, her temple, her lips, and he cupped her buttocks, practically lifting her off the floor in the process. His breath came out harsh, ragged, as the chemistry between them sizzled. There was only one way to drench their fire.

He stretched out with her in front of the fireplace as he began removing her clothes and then his. Moments later, the blaze from the fire was a flickering light across their naked skin. And then he began kissing her all over, leaving no part of her untouched, determined to quench his hunger and his desire. He had missed the taste of her and was determined to be reacquainted in every way he could think of.

"Dane..."

Her tortured moan ignited the passion within him and he leaned forward to position his body over hers, letting his throbbing erection come to rest between her thighs, gently touching the entrance of her moist heat. He lifted his head to look down at her, wanting to see her expression the exact moment their bodies joined again.

Chapter 19

Sienna stared into Dane's eyes, the heat and passion she saw in them making her shiver. The love she recognized made her heart pound, and the desire she felt for him sent surges and surges of sensations through every part of her body, especially the area between her legs, making her thighs quiver.

"You're my everything, Sienna," he whispered as he began easing inside of her. His gaze was locked with hers as his voice came out in a husky tone. "I need you like I need air to breathe, water for thirst and food for nourishment. Oh, baby, my life has been so empty since you've been gone. I love and need you."

His words touched her and when he was embedded inside of her to the hilt, she arched her back, needing and wanting even more of him. She gripped his shoulders with her fingers as liquid fire seemed to flow to all parts of her body.

And at that moment she forgot everything—the Beast from the East, their limited supply of food and the fact they were stranded together in a cabin with barely enough heat.

The only thing that registered in her mind was that they were together and expressing their love in a way that literally touched her soul.

He continued to stroke her, in and out, and with each powerful thrust into her body she moaned out his name and told him of her love. She was like a bow whose strings were being stretched to the limit each and every time he drove into her, and she met his thrusts with her own eager ones.

And then she felt it, the strength like a volcano erupting as he continued to stroke her to oblivion. Her body splintered into a thousand pieces as an orgasm ripped through her, almost snatching her breath away. And when she felt him buck, tighten his hold on her hips and thrust into her deeper, she knew that same powerful sensation had taken hold of him, as well.

"Sienna!"

He screamed her name and growled a couple of words that were incoherent to her ears. She tightened her arms around his neck, needing to be as close to him as she could get. She knew in her heart at that moment that things were going to be fine. She and Dane had proved that when it came to the power of love, it was never too late.

Sienna awoke the following morning naked, in front of the fireplace and cuddled in her husband's arms with a blanket covering them. After yawning, she raised her chin and glanced over at him and met his gaze head-on. The intensity in the dark eyes staring back at her shot heat through all parts of her body. She couldn't help but recall last night and how they had tried making up for all the time they had been apart.

"It's gone," Dane said softly, pulling her closer into his arms.

She lifted a brow. "What's gone?"

"The Beast."

She tilted her head to glance out the window and he was

right. Although snow was still falling, it wasn't the violent blizzard that had been unleashed the day before. It was as if the weather had served the purpose it had come for and had made its exit. She smiled. Evidently, someone up there knew she and Dane's relationship was meant to be saved and had stepped in to salvage it.

She was about to say something when suddenly there was a loud pounding at the door. She and Dane looked at each other, wondering who would be paying them a visit to the cabin at this hour and in this weather.

Chapter 20

Sienna, like Dane, had quickly gotten dressed and was now staring at the four men who were standing in the doorway…those handsome Steele brothers. She smiled, shaking her head. Vanessa had evidently called her cousins to come rescue her, anyway.

"Vanessa called us," Chance Steele, the oldest of the pack, said by way of explanation. "It just so happened that we were only a couple of miles down the road at our own cabin." A smile touched his lips. "She was concerned that the two of you were here starving to death and asked us to share some of our rations."

"Thanks, guys," Dane said, gladly accepting the box Sebastian Steele was handing him. "Come on in. And although we've had plenty of heat to keep us warm, I have to admit our food supply was kind of low."

As soon as the four entered, all eyes went to Sienna. Although the brothers knew Dane because their families sometimes ran in the same social circles, as well as the fact that

Dane and Donovan Steele had graduated from high school the same year, she knew their main concern was for her. She had been their cousin Vanessa's best friend for years, and as a result they had sort of adopted her as their little cousin, as well.

"You okay?" Morgan Steele asked her, although Sienna knew she had to look fine; probably like a woman who'd been made love to all night, and she wasn't ashamed of that fact. After all, Dane *was* her husband. But the Steeles knew about her pending divorce, so she decided to end their worries.

She smiled and moved closer to Dane. He automatically wrapped his arms around her shoulders and brought her closer to his side. "Yes, I'm wonderful," she said, breaking the subtle tension she felt in the room. "Dane and I have decided we don't want a divorce and intend to stay together and make our marriage work."

The relieved smiles on the faces of the four men were priceless. "That's wonderful. We're happy for you," Donovan Steele said, grinning.

"We apologize if we interrupted anything, but you know Vanessa," Chance said, smiling. "She wouldn't let up. We would have come sooner but the bad weather kept us away."

"Your timing was perfect," Dane said, grinning. "We appreciate you even coming out now. I'm sure the roads weren't their best."

"No, but my new truck managed just fine," Sebastian said proudly. "Besides, we're going fishing later. We would invite you to join us, Dane, but I'm sure you can think of other ways you'd prefer to spend your time."

Dane smiled as he glanced down and met Sienna's gaze. "Oh, yeah, I can definitely think of a few."

The power had been restored and a couple of hours later, after eating a hefty breakfast of pancakes, sausage, grits and eggs, and drinking what Dane had to admit was the best coffee he'd had in a long time, Dane and Sienna were wrapped in each other's arms in the king-size bed. Sensations flowed through her just thinking about how they had ached and hungered for each other, and the fierceness of their lovemaking to fulfill that need and greed.

"Now will you tell me what brought you to the cabin?" Sienna asked, turning in Dane's arms and meeting his gaze.

"My wedding band." He then told her why he'd come to the cabin two weeks ago and how he'd left the ring behind. "It was as if without that ring on my finger, my connection to you was gone. I had to have it back so I came here for it."

Sienna nodded, understanding completely. That was one of the reasons she hadn't removed hers. Reaching out she cupped his stubble jaw in her hand and then leaned over and kissed him softly. "Together forever, Mr. Bradford."

Dane smiled. "Yes, Mrs. Bradford, together forever. We've proved that when it comes to true love, it's never too late."

* * * * *

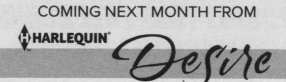
#2431 THE CEO'S UNEXPECTED CHILD
Billionaires and Babies • by Andrea Laurence
When a fertility clinic makes a mistake, a recent widow discovers her infant daughter doesn't belong to her late husband, but to a billionaire set on claiming his new family...by any means.

#2432 THE SEAL'S SECRET HEIRS
Texas Cattleman's Club: Lies and Lullabies
by Kat Cantrell
A former Navy SEAL comes home to his greatest challenge yet—surprise fatherhood of secret twins—only to discover his high school sweetheart is his children's social worker. Will the first-time father get a second shot at real love?

#2433 SNOWBOUND WITH THE BOSS
Pregnant by the Boss • by Maureen Child
When gaming tycoon Sean Ryan is stranded with irascible, irresistible contractor Kate Wells, the temptation to keep each other warm proves overwhelming. Dealing with unexpected feelings is hard enough, but what about an unexpected pregnancy? They're about to find out...

#2434 ONE SECRET NIGHT, ONE SECRET BABY
Moonlight Beach Bachelors • by Charlene Sands
Though Hollywood heartthrob Dylan McKay has no memory of that fateful night with his sister's best friend, he must face the music. He's made her pregnant and will make her his bride. But soon the shocking, unforgettable truth emerges...

#2435 THE RANCHER'S MARRIAGE PACT
Texas Extreme • by Kristi Gold
Marrying his sexy interior designer is convenient enough for rich rancher Dallas Calloway. He'll get his inheritance and she'll get a new lease on life. Then the business arrangement turns into more than they bargain for...

#2436 HIS SECRETARY'S SURPRISE FIANCÉ
Bayou Billionaires • by Joanne Rock
Winning at any cost might work on the football field, but will demanding a fake engagement really keep billionaire sportsman Dempsey Reynaud's alluring assistant in his life?

HDCNM0216

REQUEST YOUR FREE BOOKS!
2 FREE NOVELS PLUS 2 FREE GIFTS!

Ⓗ HARLEQUIN®

Desire

ALWAYS POWERFUL, PASSIONATE AND PROVOCATIVE

YES! Please send me 2 FREE Harlequin® Desire novels and my 2 FREE gifts (gifts are worth about $10). After receiving them, if I don't wish to receive any more books, I can return the shipping statement marked "cancel." If I don't cancel, I will receive 6 brand-new novels every month and be billed just $4.55 per book in the U.S. or $5.24 per book in Canada. That's a savings of at least 13% off the cover price! It's quite a bargain! Shipping and handling is just 50¢ per book in the U.S. and 75¢ per book in Canada.* I understand that accepting the 2 free books and gifts places me under no obligation to buy anything. I can always return a shipment and cancel at any time. Even if I never buy another book, the two free books and gifts are mine to keep forever.

225/326 HDN GH2P

Name _____ (PLEASE PRINT)

Address _____ Apt. #

City _____ State/Prov. _____ Zip/Postal Code

Signature (if under 18, a parent or guardian must sign)

Mail to the **Reader Service:**
IN U.S.A.: P.O. Box 1867, Buffalo, NY 14240-1867
IN CANADA: P.O. Box 609, Fort Erie, Ontario L2A 5X3

Want to try two free books from another line?
Call 1-800-873-8635 or visit www.ReaderService.com.

* Terms and prices subject to change without notice. Prices do not include applicable taxes. Sales tax applicable in N.Y. Canadian residents will be charged applicable taxes. Offer not valid in Quebec. This offer is limited to one order per household. Not valid for current subscribers to Harlequin Desire books. All orders subject to credit approval. Credit or debit balances in a customer's account(s) may be offset by any other outstanding balance owed by or to the customer. Please allow 4 to 6 weeks for delivery. Offer available while quantities last.

Your Privacy—The Reader Service is committed to protecting your privacy. Our Privacy Policy is available online at www.ReaderService.com or upon request from the Reader Service.

We make a portion of our mailing list available to reputable third parties that offer products we believe may interest you. If you prefer that we not exchange your name with third parties, or if you wish to clarify or modify your communication preferences, please visit us at www.ReaderService.com/consumerschoice or write to us at Reader Service Preference Service, P.O. Box 9062, Buffalo, NY 14240-9062. Include your complete name and address.

HD15

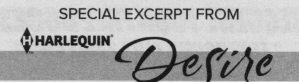
Claire looked completely panicked by the thought of Luca having access to her child.

Their child.

It seemed so wrong for him to have a child with a woman he'd never met. But now that he had a living, breathing daughter, he wasn't about to sit back and pretend it didn't happen. Eva was probably the only child he would ever have, and he'd already missed months of her life. That would not continue.

"We can and we will." Luca spoke up at last. "Eva is my daughter, and I've got the paternity test results to prove it. There's not a judge in the county of New York who won't grant me emergency visitation while we await our court date. They will say when and where and how often you have to give her to me."

Claire sat, her mouth agape at his words. "She's just a baby. She's only six months old. Why fight me for her just so you can hand her over to a nanny?"

Luca laughed at her presumptuous tone. "What makes you so certain I'll have a nanny for her?"

"You're a rich, powerful, unmarried businessman. You're better suited to run a corporation than to change a diaper. I'm willing to bet you don't have the first clue of how to care for an infant, much less the time."

Luca just shook his head and sat forward in his seat. "You know very little about me, *tesorino*, you've said so yourself, so don't presume anything about me."

Claire narrowed her gaze at him. She definitely didn't like him pushing her. And he was pushing her. Partially because he liked to see the fire in her eyes and the flush of her skin, and partially because it was necessary to get through to her.

Neither of them had asked for this to happen to them, but she needed to learn she wasn't in charge. They had to cooperate if this awkward situation was going to improve. He'd started off nice, politely requesting to see Eva, and he'd been flatly ignored. As each request was met with silence, he'd escalated the pressure. That's how they'd ended up here today. If she pushed him any further, he would start playing hardball. He didn't want to, but he would crush her like his restaurants' competitors.

"We can work together and play nice, or my lawyer here can make things very difficult for you. As he said, it's your choice."

"What are you suggesting, Mr. Moretti?" her lawyer asked.

"I'm suggesting we both take a little time away from our jobs and spend it together."

Don't miss
THE CEO'S UNEXPECTED CHILD
by Andrea Laurence, available March 2016 wherever
Harlequin® Desire books and ebooks are sold.

www.Harlequin.com

HDEXP0216

PL

Looking for more wealthy bachelors? Fear not!
Be sure to collect these sexy reads from
Harlequin® Presents and Harlequin® Blaze!

A FORBIDDEN TEMPTATION
by Anne Mather

Jack Connolly isn't looking for a woman—
until he meets Grace Spencer! Trapped in a
fake relationship to safeguard her family,
Grace knows giving in to Jack would risk
everything she holds dear… But will she
surrender to the forbidden?

Available February 16, 2016

SWEET SEDUCTION
by Daire St. Denis

When Daisy Sinclair finds out the man she
spent the night with is her ex-husband's new
lawyer, she flips. Is Jamie Forsythe in on
helping steal her family bakery? Or was their
sweet seduction the real thing?

Available March 1, 2016

HPB0216